Sweet Talkin' Sugar

Book four in the McKenna Clan Series

Christine Young

Published by Rogue Phoenix Press
Copyright © 2015

ISBN: 978-1-62420-244-5

Credits
Cover Artist: Designs by Ms G
Editor: Christie L. Kraemer

Chapter One

"Road trip!" Lyn yelled with the vibrating wind echoing through the convertible mustang before turning to slant Kimi a smile.

"Vegas here we come!" Kimi pulled out her cell phone and sticking her tongue out, took a selfie, then leaned closer to her twin and snapped another shot; this time of the two of them. "Gotta love life." She looked at Lyn, her grin contagious.

"Behave yourself, little sis." Lyn gripped the steering wheel as she watched the road fly by and enjoyed the feel of the wind whipping through her hair and the warmth of the sun on her face. They'd put the convertible top down and now had the air conditioning blaring with music revved and the volume turned to the top notch.

"I am," Lyn shot back, "behaving myself." While she pulled her hair back, fastening the white-blond strands with a hair tie. "When are we going to get there?"

"When we get there," Lyn said deadpan, keeping her gaze focused on the road ahead. Her mind spun in
different directions, her skin suddenly prickling and a shadow of apprehension filling her soul. Thoughts of Jokul, the Ice Demon and the Amazonian Devil, rattled in her head. She unexpectedly had serious feelings about this trip and they were all negative. Where they came from, she couldn't fathom. When they left Tahoe, the plan seemed to be a good one but now, on the road, she wasn't sure why she'd chosen this route. If she could

convince her twin, Kimi, to drive through Vegas and keep going to the Sierra Madres, she would. Her gut told her trouble waited even while she couldn't put a finger on what exactly that concern entailed. She wanted nothing more than to go home.

"You don't have to be so grumpy." Kimi pulled her knees up to her chest and let her head rest on the back of the seat. "Don't you want to go to Vegas any more? It was your idea, you know? I just wanted to keep you company. Guess the roles have been reversed."

"You read me like an open book," Lyn told her sister with a sheepish grin. "I did, but now I don't." She shrugged, "What can I say? My animal instincts have taken over and I feel a dark cloud of foreboding hovering over the city."

"I see." Kimi sat up and stared at Lyn. "What's bothering you? You're not usually a doomsayer?" Her voice took on a somber tone.

"A sixth sense."

"All right. And what does this strange feeling tell you?" Kimi questioned, her brows furrowed together.

Lyn darted a quick look at Kimi, whose expression told Lyn that Kimi took her seriously. "Nothing and that's the problem, but my gut tells me we won't be happy if we go through Vegas. I feel shivers creep down my spine every time I think or say the name of that city."

Kimi let out a long and a very dramatic sigh. "And I was so looking forward to trying my hand at blackjack in Sin City."

Lyn chuckled softly. "Your five dollar bet wouldn't get you very far. Are there any granola bars left in the snack sack?"

"Don't change the subject and no, I ate the last one a mile back." Her voice rising with anticipated excitement, she said, "You know I could double it. If I made money, I'd let myself keep playing."

"If you doubled your money, you'd quit. You and I both know that's they way you gamble." Lyn swerved a little to miss a tumbleweed dancing along the road before concentrating on her thoughts and doubts.

"Sure is hot."

"You're changing the subject, Kimi. Is the conversation getting a little too heated for you to handle?"

"No, I just don't know what to say to you when you're always right." Kimi sent a smirk Lyn's way, pushing a strand of hair from her face.

Ignoring Kimi's insinuation that she was always right, Lyn thrummed her fingers on the wheel, humming along with the tune on the radio all the while trying to ignore the warnings the voice in her head kept tossing out. "Let's compromise. We can stay tonight, gamble a little and maybe take in a show if someone we like is performing. I'd like to be on our way home in the morning."

The next few hours passed in relative silence. Kimi had leaned back in the seat, eyes closed and faking sleep. Lyn enjoyed the silence, not wanting to voice any more of her fears to Kimi. They had just experienced the ice demon, Jokul and only a year before had encountered an Amazonian Devil who nearly killed her. She had every right to be cautious.

She didn't want or need any more demons to come after her or anyone in her family. Relaxing, soaking up the sun's rays, and a little vitamin D was on her mind. But she didn't think that was going to happen anytime soon. Getting out of Dodge, or in this case Vegas, was at the top of her list of to dos.

The desert was a place Lyn loved; the color, the dry air, and the storms. God, but she loved the thunderstorms when they swept across the hills. She loved Infinity Cliff and enjoyed the silence when she dropped a stone from the top. She'd been away far too long.

It was past time to go home.

Cactus Junction; she didn't believe any town had been named more appropriately. Somehow she believed her future would be revealed soon, and she hoped it would happen in the Sierra Madres, at Cactus Junction, or maybe at the top of Infinity Cliff.

The dreams had returned; the surreal imaginings of her mind while sleeping. Somehow she knew her soul mate had been in them, had spoken to her and given her encouragement when she lay on her deathbed after tangling with the Amazonian Devil: Chullachaqui.

When darkness cloaked her and she lay in her great grandfather's sweat lodge, Carr had sat by her side and it was Carr's hands that had healed her physical wounds. But it was the dark haired stranger with sharp rugged features who had spoken to her with calm reassurance who healed her soul. He didn't leave her side until she regained consciousness and now she didn't know if she'd ever see him or hear his voice again.

Her family could tell her about the dream and its meaning, but she'd never had the courage to approach them. Now after battling a new foe, Jokul, she had to talk to someone. Nigan, her great grandfather, was the logical choice for a conversation. And she wondered, too, if she had another power. Carr could heal and was head of the McKenna clan worldwide. Brody was the head of the clan in the Sierra Madres.

Lyn chuckled to herself. Carr had always thought he would live life with no responsibilities only to find himself burdened with the greatest of all. But he was capable and wise. Carr would do well with his new position.

"Are we almost there?" Kimi sat up, rubbing her eyes then stretching her back and arms. "I'd love a cheeseburger and fries."

"About ten minutes away." Lyn slanted a quick look at her twin. "And we can stop for food anytime. Personally, I'd preferred something a bit more healthy."

"Slammin'. I've got my five bucks handy." She pulled out her wallet and brought out a five-dollar bill. "I'm set."

"Brody made us reservations at Caesar's Palace. He left it open-ended. Said we could decide how long we wanted to pay for it. For now let's plan on one night. If things go well, we can always stay another night."

"One night, but that's okay as long as your willing to consider staying longer." Kimi paused, "Why don't I have the same super power you do? We are twins."

Lyn sighed, wishing she could really look at the expression on Kimi's face. "We aren't anything the same so why should we have the same power, save shifting? We will discover our second power soon enough. Sometimes I think it's the ability to annoy with words."

"I know, I know, we've been through this before. I like to stay home and cook and by the way, that wasn't very nice."

"I'm sorry. You know I love you."

"Apology accepted. You can be annoying too. No matter the topic, you're always right."

"I like to hunt and you don't." Lyn ignored the last comment.

"I'd rather read a good book," Kimi sighed.

"And I love adventure and the thrill of the chase."

"The list goes on and we both understand we are total opposites." Kimi pulled on her seatbelt.

"I don't hold that against you." Lyn laughed. "If we were the same we'd compete against each other. Now we just make each other whole."

"How did you get so smart?"

Lyn didn't know how to respond to that question. They were both highly intelligent, but Kimi always had a feeling she was less competent. She hated the self-doubt her twin felt in her accomplishments and talents.

"Like I said, we make each other whole, compliment each other."

"I just wish I was more like you," Kimi said.

"And sometimes I wish I was more like you."

"Yeah, when?" Kimi demanded.

"That one is easy. Every time I dash off on some wild adventure and end up regretting the act."

Kimi placed her hand on Lyn's arm. "I know you still regret going after the Amazonian Devil."

"Yes, except for the fact that if I had stayed home as I promised, Sadie wouldn't be with us and Brody would be one very unhappy man."

Traffic picked up as they drew closer to the city and the sun hung on the hills about to disappear behind them. One night and she'd have to give Kimi some time to explore the insides of the hotels in Vegas. Venturing outside on the sidewalks was always interesting, but an adventure she could do without.

City lights glittered brightly. If anything, Vegas was filled with lights and people—the energy electrifying the night air. Adrenalin seemed to fill every nook and cranny of the vibrant city.

"I heard that." Kimi laughed at the sound of Lyn's stomach rumbling. "We didn't stop for lunch and I'm hungry too. Where do you want to eat?"

"Let's get settled in then we can look around the casinos. What are you in the mood for?"

"Italiano..."

"Sounds good to me." Lyn drove into a parking place and turning off the car's engine, she left Kimi to babysit their stuff. "I'll be back in a second. Don't go anywhere."

A few minutes later, Kimi flopped on the bed in their room and kicked off her shoes. "Maybe I don't care if we explore the casinos and gamble. I'm exhausted."

"No, you don't. We're going to find food and spend your five dollars. If we don't, I'm going to hear about it for the next six months." Despite the fact Lyn wanted nothing more than a hot shower and a good night's sleep before starting for Cactus Junction tomorrow afternoon, she knew Kimi needed to unwind. Perhaps she did too. So what would a couple of days do to her gut? She felt a slow curl of ice inside. Risking the extra time could put her life or Kimi's on the line.

"All right," Kimi said. "Let's do it. Let's eat then find a slot machine that wants to take my pennies."

"I think the slots just take dollars, honey."

"Oh, well, five won't go very far unless I win the first round. If that's the case, we can be out of here in the a.m. instead of the p.m." She grinned. "And what are the odds of that?"

Lyn turned to her side, propping her head up with a hand and grinning. "I'm feeling better about this sojourn in Vegas. Let's change our clothes and see what damage we can do in the casino."

"I'm game." Kimi skipped to her suitcase and after opening it, rummaged through the contents until she came up for air with a pair of skinny jeans and a dark blue halter-top. She held it up for Lyn's scrutiny and with Lyn's nod, she headed for the bathroom. "Going to take a quick shower then it's your turn."

~ * ~

In observation mode, he walked through the casino, hands in his pockets, listening and watching, his heart racing. Before the blackjack table at the end of the row, he paused to reflect and decide on a course of action. The air inside was sultry, hot and smoke-filled. He swept one hand through his damp hair, fresh from a summer rain. He forced his mind from the heat and the rancid smell of cigarettes, and with single-minded focus, stared at the table and the cards lying innocuously on the green felt.

The picture of cool calmness, she sat on a bar stool, a drink in hand and cards in the other, her legs crossed provocatively. Her daringly cut emerald V-neck dress didn't leave much to the imagination, but he forced his gaze to the man beyond who stared at her as if he owned her. Every hair on the back of his neck stood on end and a chill slivered down his spine, nerves on edge, muscles tensed. His brows furrowed when the man turned his attention, for one brief moment, his way.

The dealer gave her another card and she tipped one corner up to look at it then let it go. Her body language spoke volumes to him and he wondered if the dealer noticed too. The poker face she so obviously tried for was something she'd never possess.

Deacon McClain paused before settling on a bar stool across the table from her. He waited for the last hand to finish before placing his chips in front of him and nodding to the dealer he was ready to play. His fingers closed around his glass of whiskey as his heart thundered in his chest. She glanced his way, inquisitively cocking her head to one side before slanting him a sexy-as-hell-grin.

The grin sent a message that nearly catapulted him from his seat. Inhaling a deep breath to calm his splintering nerves, he turned his attention back to the cards he'd just been dealt. Not good, not good at all, he motioned for another, then sat back and gazed at Lyonesse. Lyn McKenna, the woman he'd been sent to find and bring home. He'd never believed this gig to be an easy one, but now he felt sure this might be his most difficult assignment of all. Her easy grin sent his heart into a tailspin and her long shapely legs were hard to ignore. What would happen if she gave him her full attention?

He'd lose all sense of perspective and balance.

Hours passed in a blur. He won and lost. Smoke blurred his senses and the whiskey could have dulled them, but he wasn't drinking. The girl seemed to have a winning streak going. Her twin stopped by every once in a while to talk and laugh, then she'd wander off in some direction only to reappear, usually with another drink.

He looked at his watch before twirling his untouched whiskey around in his glass, "Two a.m."

Kimi, her twin, rested a hand on her sister's shoulder. After a huge yawn she asked, "I'm turning in for the night. You comin'?"

"Not yet." Lyn's gaze swept the room, stopping for a second on him. Her brows furrowed as if she had thoughts she wasn't sure of, as if she recognized him.

Kimi gave her sister a heavy sigh. "Don't stay up too late. I know you wanted to get an early start tomorrow."

So they weren't staying long. He'd have to work fast then follow the pair. He was pretty sure they were heading to her home and Cactus Junction was a place he'd like to see if he had all the time in the world. But he didn't think that was the case.

He leaned back, letting the dealer take his cards and chips. She nodded for another hand and he declined. For the first time that night, Lyn turned her full attention his way, a frown suddenly marring her gorgeous features. She squinted her eyes as if studying him.

The look was so intense and so inquisitive he wanted to laugh, but he held the emotion in check. Instead, he saluted her with his glass of whiskey and was rewarded with a nod and an expression he didn't know how to read.

A cloying scent penetrated the room despite the lingering odor of smoke and his mind spiraled in another direction. A large man wearing jeans and a black pinstriped suit jacket moved closer to Lyn. The man tipped his Stetson before nodding to a waitress to bring her a drink. Standing behind Lyn, the man waited, shifting from one foot to the other, his gaze roaming the room to return every few seconds to Lyn.

Lyn shook her head at the drink before a shuttered expression crossed her face. "No thanks." Her shoulder trembled and her back stiffened as if to stop whatever sensation that was racing through her body.

"I insist." The man's gravelly voice reverberated back hundreds of generations. He shifted from one foot to the other then wiped his forehead with the back of his hand.

"No!" Lyn pushed the recently dealt cards back to the dealer and gathering her chips, rose. "I'm done."

Deacon's heart raced and he clasped his fingers into fists in anticipation of a possible fight.

The man's eyebrows drew together, his lips thinning his large body blocking her path. "You'll stay and have a drink with me."

"Or what?" Not waiting for an answer, she turned to walk away but the man stopped her, placing his hand on her shoulder and yanking her backwards toward him.

She shook it off as Deacon bolted from his chair, slamming his shoulder into the man's chest. "Go!" he told Lyn while keeping his gaze focused on the man. "Go now."

From the corner of his vision, he watched Lyn stop, hands fisted at her sides as if she meant to fight this gigantic man. He realized she wasn't going to take orders from him either, at least not yet. Inwardly, he grinned.

The man hit him in the face, pushing him against the blackjack table. He dropped, slipping to the side to gain room to move. Drunken gamblers cheered them, encouraging the altercation, shouting advice.

Deacon calculated, running toward him, tackling the man and sending him to the floor. The two rolled across the ground sending blows against each other. He hit the man's nose then the side of his head. Patrons moved back, scattering away and giving them room.

In the next moment, the man pushed from him and sprinted through the casino doors to the outside. Deacon rose, watching the man run before dusting off his clothing, he looked for Lyn. Hightailin' it out of here was not such a bad idea, but security guards who had suddenly surrounded him had a different idea.

Explaining his actions wasn't possible. What part of, "He'd just saved Lyn McKenna from Balor, the demonic God of Death, who was chasing her" would they believe? He shrugged, "Sorry about that. Didn't like the way he looked at my girl." He turned to Lyn and winked, hoping she'd go along with his statement. But the look on her face didn't bode well. She wasn't the type to be suckered in with a wink and a grin.

"A..." Lyn began, then slanted the guards an earth stopping smile. Her baby blue eyes twinkled with what looked like mischief.

"I'll pay for the damage." He interrupted, pulling out a wad of cash and after taking several hundreds from his money clip; he slipped his arm through Lyn's and said. "Let's get out of here, Sugar."

She seemed to comply, playing along with the charade he'd just created, but when they reached the hall, she pulled away and slapped him across the cheek. He brought his hand up to touch the fiery spot where she'd connected. "What was that for?" He expected her to tell him he was crazy.

"Don't sugar, me!" Her eyes blazed with fury, her body shaking. She stepped backward, stumbling against a potted plant.

Without another word and with head held high, she strode away from him toward the elevator. "You're not going anywhere without me, Sugar." He didn't want to address the issue of the nickname that had popped from his mouth. A nickname that fit her beautifully.

She didn't turn or stop, and when she reached the lift, she pushed the up button several times as if the repeated gesture would move it along at a faster pace. He watched her inhale a deep breath and stiffen her spine as she waited. Her toe began to tap the marble floor.

Not wanting to intrude, yet knowing he had to find a way to convince her to go with him, he caught up with her and stepped into the elevator when the doors opened. He half expected another slap across the face, but she moved to the opposite side of the tiny box and focused her attention on the panel.

Christine Young

"You won't get there any faster if you punch that little round metal thing a hundred times," he said, crossing his arms and leaning against the shiny wall. God, how he wanted to tell her everything, but he didn't know what she'd think. He knew she was a shifter so she had to believe in the paranormal, but what he needed to tell her was beyond believable even for a shifter.

"No, but it makes me feel better. What is it you want?" Her hands rested on her hips and he thought he saw a quirk of an almost smile before her brows furrowed together in a look of displeasure. "I don't know what you just protected me from down there in the casino, but I might need defending from you too, so stay out of my way."

You; I want you.

"I need to tell you some things and I want to get you out of Vegas before the Neanderthal I just fought realizes you're staying in this hotel. I can't tell you everything, but your life is in danger."

"Danger? Talk."

Deacon took off his and ruffed his hair, wishing he could think of an easier way to tell her how much peril she was in. "Your life is at stake. There are creatures...men who want you..."

"You're not telling me anything I haven't guessed at. That man gave me the creeps. How do I know you aren't the creature I need to run from?"

"You don't know, but I think you've seen me before in your dreams, and if you recall, I watched over you once before when your life was in jeopardy. That fact should give you a tiny bit of confidence in me. I wish we had the time to spend and I'd tell you everything. For now, you need to trust me and in your instincts." He prayed her gut was telling her he wasn't her enemy.

She stiffened and an expression crossed her face, one he wasn't sure how to read. "My brother, Carr healed me. I don't know anything about you and I don't think I want to know."

"Pretty little liar. But I need for you to take what I tell you seriously. I want you to leave with me now, before you go to your room. Kimi is not in jeopardy, and your presence with her only puts her in peril."

11

"That's quite the pick-up line. Come with me, your life is in danger. Really?" She jabbed the elevator button again. "Really?"

"That man I fought wants your life in exchange for his. Do I need to say more? He made a deal with a pack of devils." Frustration beat in his head and he searched for words to convince Lyn, but couldn't think of anything. Trust didn't come easy for shifters and Lyn was no exception.

"Yes. Talk."

He held up his hands in a gesture of submission. "I don't have the words to make you trust. Look inside your heart and your soul, close your eyes and breathe in my essence. That should be enough to tell you I don't mean you harm." He felt as if he groped for the words and thoughts even as time flew by and danger sped closer.

"Just for the record, I don't trust you." This time she pushed the down button that would take them back to the ground floor. "But I don't want to put Kimi's life on the line."

"You believe me." The question hung heavy for a few tense moments as the elevator slid down the shaft.

"My gut says you're telling the truth as does my heart." The doors opened and she stepped into the lobby of the hotel. "I'm going to leave Kimi a message. I don't want her to worry."

He followed, pushing the hat he wore back on his forehead. "All ready took care of that, Sugar." Deacon watched her jaw tighten when he used the term of endearment. Best she'd get used to it; he planned on callin' her Sugar for a long time, a lifetime and perhaps longer.

"You take liberties that aren't yours to take. Damn you! I'm going to leave her a message anyway. How do I know what you said in the note you left?" She marched toward the lobby desk.

"All you have to do is ask. Oh, I forgot, you don't trust me."

"No, I don't." She turned to look over her shoulder at him.

His heart lurched. "Look, I wouldn't have done it if we'd had all the time in the world, but we don't. You have to come with me *now*." The cloying scent of seawater and dead fish he'd recognized earlier filtered in through the front door.

She turned to the desk, but he lifted her in his arms and strode to the exit door while she beat on his shoulders and screamed for him to put her down. The one person in the lobby turned to stare, but at three a.m. even in Vegas there weren't very many people in the area. They were all in the casinos or their rooms.

Once inside the empty stairwell, he told her, "Hold on tight, Sugar. We're going for a ride. This is going to rock your world." His body tensed and all his senses focused on teleporting.

As the walls began to whirl, slowly at first then picking up speed as the world turned and spun, he felt her fingers bite into his muscles. "Good girl," he whispered then as suddenly as it had begun, the churning stopped.

Deacon held on to Lyn while her body adjusted to the warp speed travel. Her heart thundered against his ribs while he cradled her tight, her face tucked into his shoulder.

When they settled to a stop, Lyn pulled away from him, smoothing her skirt and readjusting the top to make sure all of her was covered. "Shit! What just happened?"

How do you tell someone she just traveled through thin air? "We teleported." His voice shook with fear for her and simmering emotions she must feel. This tiny diversion would not stop the demonic creature that had just been unleashed, raised from the dead.

"That's what Margo and Phaedra did to save my family, but they used a crystal. You just did it. By yourself. On your own. With no help." Her voice shuddered. "Put me down."

"Only if you promise not to go anywhere." He set her on her feet but kept his hands around her waist. "And don't look down."

The last sentence came too late as Lyn stumbled. "Where the hell are we? Who the hell are you?"

Deacon caught her before she fell off the cliff. "Uh...mountains... Deacon's my name. Deacon McClain at your service, Sugar." He couldn't tell her the mountain was pure illusion and if she did step off the other side, she'd be on hard sand. He still didn't want her to fall, she could still hurt herself, twist an ankle and a myriad of other possible injuries flew through his mind.

"I'm not your, Sugar. God, I should be more concerned about where we are and what you want with me. And what you're not telling me."

If only I could tell you the truth, but you wouldn't believe me if I did. "Listen, the truth will come out in time. Right now we're going to wait for your sister to give us a lift then..."

"A lift? Here? We're a couple thousand feet from the ground, and I don't see a road anywhere." She looked from side to side then down.

"It's an illusion."

"What the f--"

He held up a hand in hopes of stopping the tirade before it began. "I've created a fantasy to keep you safe. No one, not even Balor, can see us here. I will see the lights from your sister's car when she nears and I'll signal her to stop."

"Balor?"

Lyn let out a long breath of air, and he sensed she was frustrated because of what he wasn't telling her. "I must keep the man I fought in the casino away from you."

"I can defend myself."

"Not against him, at least, not until you have all the information. Besides, I'd rather you didn't have to fight any battles." He knew she was a shifter but she was still female and even in her jaguar form she wasn't as strong as a male. God, but he remembered the dream vigil he'd spent over her bed when the Amazonian Devil had nearly killed her and his hands shook with the fear something like that might happen again.

"You're not my keeper. What kind of battle is supposedly coming my way?" She was backing up, shaking her head, hands out as if to ward him off.

"I'd rather speak of it someplace where you can sit down comfortably." He reached for her, trying to stop her backward travel.

"Ok, ok." She sat down, pulling her knees to her chin and wrapping her arms around her legs. "Talk."

"This is not what I had in mind." He prayed her sister would show up soon. Despite the fact Lyn couldn't locate a road; they were only about ten feet from the highway. He saw it and in his mind he counted the seconds until he could lift the cloaking from around the boulder.

"There appears to be time." She smoothed the fabric of her dress before changing position and wrapping her arms around herself to ward off the chill off the early morning.

Slipping his arms from his jacket, he wrapped it around her shoulders and sat down next to her. "I watched over you when the Amazonian devil nearly killed you. Wasn't very smart of you to try to take on a man's job."

As soon as the words were out of his mouth, he regretted them. It wasn't exactly what he meant, but it was so close to the truth, he couldn't deny his feelings and the emotions he'd felt when he saw her lying so still and near death. He didn't have much experience dealing with a woman who could fight a man's battles and live to tell about it. In his clan, the women weren't shifters. He didn't know any women who were, save Lyn and Kimi.

He heard Lyn's swift intake of air, and against his side he felt her stiffen. When he looked at her face, her eyes shimmered with unspoken anger. "What do you know about the Amazonian Devil?"

A brief and probably short-lived reprieve from his chauvinistic statement gave him a confidence to proceed. Taming her fury seemed prudent. "I watched over you until you were healed. I sat by your bed next to Carr and your grandfather."

"Carr healed me and you weren't there. My brother and my grandfather would have spoken of you." Her defenses were charged. She wasn't going to let him get away with half truths and subtle innuendos.

"Now listen closely. I don't take any credit for healing your body, but there was more damage to you than just physical. I stayed with you. Don't you remember any of it? I know I was part of your dreams."

She turned to look at him, pulling the jacket close and pushing hair from her face. She faced him but her eyes were closed as if she was trying to keep him from seeing inside her soul. "I do remember a dark haired man, talking to me, encouraging me, but I don't recall that it was your face."

His heart fell. "Guess I didn't leave much of an impact."

She made a noise. "Someone made an impression. I'm just not sure it was you and if it was you..." her voice trailed off. Thin desert air circled around them as an owl hooted in the darkness of the night.

He needed to finish the sentence for her but declined, knowing that even if, on some philosophical level she believed in soul mates, this was too soon to tell her who he was and he wasn't sure he believed the ancient stories himself. He'd just hinted at it and now he didn't want to take two steps forward only to land five steps back in this relationship.

"Let me tell you a story."

"Really? You want to tell stories when you just dropped a bomb in my lap? You're a shifter. Why can't you just say it?"

"Yes I am. But not the same as you..."

"Your other form is a cat. It would be really weird..."

"I'm a white tiger."

"Albino, like me?"

"Yes..." He wasn't sure what to say. She understood and had heard the lore of the clans. McKennas didn't keep the members of the clan innocent of knowledge and she had two older brothers.

"So, what's this tall tale that you're itchin' to tell?" Lyn looked at him with a wide-eyed innocence he'd never seen before.

"You've got the most beautiful blue eyes I have ever seen, Sugar."

Fool.

"And you have the most sheepish look I have ever seen. Don't understand why you want to call me Sugar. And you can nix the come-ons. I won't fall for them. I wasn't born yesterday."

He caught sight of lights in the distance. "We'll finish this later. Your sister is here."

Lyn put her hand up to her eyes. "I don't see anything."

Deacon rose and swept his hand from right to left. The cloaking device lifted and the roar of a car could be heard.

Lyn stood and grabbed his arm. "That's not our car."

"It's okay, I rented a different one. The man who is after you could have found out what the two of you were driving."

"He could find out what you rented."

Deacon shook his head. "Don't think so." He jumped from the rock before holding a hand out to help Lyn.

Ignoring the hand and his attempt at a peace treaty, she stepped down and waited for Kimi.

As the Ferrari pulled to a stop, Deacon leaned over and asked, "what took you so long?"

Kimi stared at the once stranded couple, a grin on her face. "Had to figure out how to drive this thing. And there was this strange guy who kept watching me."

~ * ~

"Lyonesse is the sacrifice needed to appease the Fomori. I have to capture her and bring her to my people." Balor mumbled as he paced the tiny shack where he'd set up camp deep in the mountains. The encounter with the shifter had left him shaken and in need of sleep, but with the bright moonlight and the wind whistling through the rafters, sleep proved elusive.

"Fuck, I'm tired. Perhaps death was preferable to this. The fee I have to pay is too much, too damn much. When I was dead, I was at peace. I was never hungry or tired. Why the hell did I want to live again?" His grumbling stomach set his nerves jumping. Every whistle of wind and animal noise sent chills down his back.

Because my memories were better than reality. Because I thought life had cheated me. Because...

When he'd arrived at his base camp, he'd ripped the mask he'd been wearing from his face. Sweat ran down his cheeks and his neck to pool in the collar band of his shirt. His single gigantic eye in the middle of his forehead absorbed the brightness of the light. He squinted then, blinking a couple of times, let his vision adjust.

He didn't know where Deacon McClain would hide her. Could be Cactus Junction, but that was just too predictable. If McClain was anything, it wasn't predictable. He could take her to the McClain home. In either case she'd be protected by shifters: a whole clan of them. Even though he could kill people by staring at them with his one eye, it didn't seem to have the same affect on paranormal creatures.

The Fomori had been adamant about their fee. The sacrificial victim had to be Lyn McKenna, no other would do. He didn't get why. He'd brought the demons who had freed him two virgins. They'd sacrificed the girls but they still wanted the McKenna chick. Something about her other power that had them foaming at the mouth. Hell, if he guessed right, Lyn didn't know what her second power was either; that or she didn't know how to use it. When she learned, she'd be a formidable foe. She had telekinetic powers, could move things with her thoughts. He'd felt that power when he'd seen her in the casino.

Lord, but she'd had several opportunities while he'd stalked her. She couldn't know or she had incredible strength of will. Not to send a vase hurtling across a room just for the hell of it, would take more strength than he could render. She'd done nothing even though he'd thought he'd provoked her several times.

His stomach rumbled hungrily and his head ached from lack of food. *Peace,* he'd give just about anything for one moment of solitude without pain. He strode to the meager counter in the kitchen and rummaging through the cupboards found a bottle of whiskey and an empty jar of peanut butter. Not bothering to pour a glass, he drank straight from the bottle, chugging the liquid as if it were water.

The grinding ache in the pit of his stomach didn't go away with the liquor. Pulling down a box of crackers, he stuffed several in his mouth before swallowing another shot. With both hands on the counter he leaned forward, hanging his head, frustration and shame eating at his insides. This bargain was unholy and deceitful, but he'd thought he'd be happier alive than dead.

Thoughts of his son, Lug, swept through him. Fuck, but his son had killed him, shot him with his slingshot. His fuckin' son killed him.

Fuck.

A lone tear trickled down his cheek, then another. The tears turned to gut wrenching sobs. He brushed the hated moisture away with the back of his hand and stiffened, more determined than ever to bring Lyn McKenna to the monsters so he could be set free.

Fuck! He was the demonic God of Death. Tears shouldn't fall. He caused pain to anyone who stood in his way, not the other way around.

His stomach gurgled and protested the crackers and whiskey. He clutched his neck as if that gesture could hold back the bile that burned in his throat. Running to the back door, he made it just in time and hurled on the bushes beside the back porch. Wiping his mouth with his sleeve, he sat on the steps and stared into the darkness, more tears sliding down his cheeks.

Where were they? Where did McClain take her? And how would he find out where the happy couple had gone?

He'd go crazy trying to find them; the world was huge. He could kill people with his one eye just by staring at them, but he couldn't read minds and he didn't have a damn GPS system planted on Lyn McKenna's body.

If he wanted, he could leave a path of dead bodies in his wake, but he couldn't bring one damn shape shifter to the Fomori for sacrifice.

His stomach moaned in distress. He hadn't eaten for days—save crackers and whiskey.

There was a mom-pop grocery down the road. He needed to get food, something more filling than saltines and alcohol. When he'd driven by the first time, he thought about stopping, but he'd been so damn on edge he couldn't think straight. He had a few coins and could have bought a candy bar or a frozen dinner.

Maybe with food in his belly and a night's sleep he'd be able to think.

Ten minutes later he stood outside the closed grocery store, threading his fingers through the fake hair attached to his mask. He knew what he had to do; get in and get out with out anyone noticing. A place like this wouldn't have an alarm system. Fuck, but he'd been caught once before and nearly jumped out of his skin when the blaring started. With any luck, the people here wouldn't know until morning that anyone had robbed them. Drool spilled from his lips as he thought of food.

Luck wasn't on his side; when he stepped inside, the alarm pounded in his ears. He grabbed a couple of candy bars and two bags of cookies before sprinting for his jeep. With a roar and a cloud of dust he barreled onto the road and in the opposite direction from his shack, thinking that if anyone saw him leave they wouldn't know he was planning on doubling back. He wanted to retrieve his whiskey.

Whiskey cleared his head and helped him sleep. It made him feel better from the inside out. When he felt better, he could concentrate on the girl.

Chapter Two

"You don't think whoever is following me won't have a GPS planted in your car?" Lyn watched Kimi climb into the tiny back seat, making room for her to sit in the front. It wasn't like either of them to follow blindly, but this situation seemed different—urgent in a strange way.

And they were both used to the unpredictable.

"Are you Deacon?" Kimi made a face at her sister but didn't say anything for a few minutes. "Wasn't too sure what to make of your note or the car, but the fact you had my sister told me I had to follow your list of 'to dos.' Now tell me, are you good or are you bad?"

"Thanks," Deacon said, "Much obliged. This time I'm the good guy." Deacon cleared his throat then gunned the car after slanting, what Lyn was getting used to seeing, Kimi a mischievous smile.

"This time?" Kimi asked, raising one eyebrow in speculation. "I'm not sure I like the sound of that.

"Where are we going now?" Lyn plopped down on the front seat, crossing her arms in front of her. She didn't like Deacon McClain's high handedness, but something in her heart told her this was for the best.

Looking at his profile, her body melted. His chiseled features and bronzed skin made him appear ruggedly handsome. He was her kind of guy and that thought frightened her. He was the type she always fell for and in the end 'her type' always hurt her. Apprehension slithered through her yet the sensations weren't cold. Somehow, she felt his presence and knew he would always be good for her.

"We are headed to Boulder City, Nevada. I've sent a message to Brody McKenna and he will have his private jet waiting to take Kimi home." His fingers tightened around the steering wheel and nervous energy seemed to bounce around his aura. Electric currents charged the air.

Lyn felt the absence of oxygen for a short second.

"What about Lyn?" Kimi's voice was urgent and from the back seat, demanding an answer. "I'm not leaving without her. We stick together. Thick and thin. Together forever."

"Yes, you are. Lyn is going with me to a place where she'll be safe." Deacon braked for a corner before accelerating. "And before you ask..."

"Where is that?" Kimi leaned forward, her fingers digging into Lyn's shoulder. "Where are you taking my twin, my other half?"

"It's all going to work out. Don't worry."

Kimi relaxed her fingers. Lyn let her head fall on the back seat of the car, listening to the conversation, yet feeling detached from it all. Somehow, she knew she had no voice in what was happening to her and she understood Brody had played a role in the decision-making. Going along with their plan would be the easiest task, but she had to protest at least once.

"If I told you, she might not be safe," Deacon answered back. "If you know, you might let it slip or inadvertently tell someone. I won't take that chance. I'm not going to let anything that might hurt Lyn into her life."

Deciding she'd had enough, yet wishing for a few moments of peace, she intended to speak her mind. Knowing her thoughts didn't count; she straightened and turned her attention to both Kimi and Deacon, "Stop it. Both of you," Lyn said. "You all are talking as if I'm not here. I've a choice in all this and I'm not going with you." She breathed deeply. Courage wasn't forthcoming, but she sure as hell needed strength right now. Rubbing her face with her hands, she closed her eyes and tried to think things through.

Ignoring her declaration, Deacon sat back and drove without talking. The hum of the motor soothed her nerves, but Lyn knew her little denouncement wasn't going to change Deacon's mind. He'd have to hog tie her to get her to go with him. But the memory of his arms scooping her up and the rapid teleport blasted her nerves raw. God, he was like a wrecking ball battering down her defenses. She'd never felt quite so helpless in her life. Even when her big brothers played guardian and nursemaid to her, she didn't she feel so helpless. Dependence was not a feeling she wanted to consume her. Yet maybe relying on someone besides her brothers was not such a bad idea.

Silence raffled through the car. She reached over and turned on the radio. "I can't stand all this noise," she said, wishing now for a break from her thoughts and once again searching for the peace she desperately needed.

Deacon let out a loud laugh. "Like your humor, Sugar."

Lyn wanted to rail at him for using his pet name for her in front of her sister, but she was starting to like the way his voice turned tender and sweet when he said it.

"What? No recriminations?" He laughed again, looking at her for a brief moment before turning his attention back to the highway.

"Not this time, honey. I'm too tired to object."

"You're starting to like me." His lazy grin seemed to stretch across his face.

She bristled and smoothed her skirt before answering. "I didn't say that."

From the back seat, Kimi said, "I think it's cute, but how do you two know each other well enough to have nicknames for each other and such terms of endearment?"

Deacon and Lyn glanced at each other, then Lyn turned back to watch the road. *Terms of endearment?* Was that how his words sounded? She couldn't fathom where this was coming from or that it was happening so soon.

She too wondered where he was taking her. Someplace safe he'd said, but wouldn't that be in Cactus Junction where her brothers would surround her and shield her from any evil coming her way? They wouldn't let anyone get close. And wouldn't it be better to draw this demon out rather than hide from him?

"I still think someone should know where you're taking Lyn." Kimi's voice rang out from the back seat.

Deacon stopped whistling to the tune playing on the radio. "Brody will know. If he chooses to tell you, he will. This isn't up to me yet."

"What do you mean, yet?" Lyn turned to stare at the side of Deacon's face, a soft spot for this shifter forming in her soul. She liked the clean cut of his features, the muscles cording his neck and shoulder. He took one hand off the steering wheel and took her hand in his.

"I'm not sure you're ready to hear what I have to say, and I'm not sure I believe it either." He squeezed her hand before letting it go. "But someday..." he hesitated, "someday we both might understand what I'm trying to say and until then..."

"Try me. I'm not known for my patience." The challenge echoed in the night air and seemed to bounce off the walls of the car.

Deacon braked, slowing for the three deer crossing the road in front of them. "Too much at stake." His words were clipped. "Too soon to tell. Only when the time is right."

"Listen to me," Lyn began, "if I'm going to follow you blindly, I need to feel some measure of trust and at the moment, I don't know what to feel. I'm not used to the likes of you and the way you handle every situation. I'm coming down from a whirlwind adventure in Lake Tahoe and hoping for some relaxation. This is not what the doctor prescribed."

"You can trust me. I promise you and maybe where we are going we'll have some time to relax and get to know each other."

"Words," Kimi said from the backseat. "Just words."

"She's right. I haven't known you long enough to depend on you or your judgment."

"Time will tell," Kimi added.

"Unfortunately, we don't have that pleasure. Time." Deacon turned off the highway, following the directions to the airport.

Lyn wiped her sweaty hands down her skirt, smoothing the fabric and wishing she had something else to wear. She thought of her suitcase, which Kimi must have packed. "This is it then? Did you bring my clothes?"

"Didn't have the time for that. You know, I should go with you guys," Kimi said. "Don't want to leave if my sister...if she might be in danger."

"She is in danger, but there is no way I can take both of you." Deacon's tone was matter-of-fact.

Lyn remembered the teleport, "What, you're not strong enough to hold both of us in your arms?" She didn't like the sound of her voice and the sarcasm coating her words. It wasn't like her to act this way but at the moment every inch of her body trembled.

"You're trying to provoke me and it's not going to work. I understand the fear and the frustration, but Kimi will help you more by staying in Cactus Junction. She's your shield and your salvation. She knows you better than anyone."

"How?" Both girls asked.

"Balor will look for you first at your home and then mine if he survives the confrontation with your brothers. If he sees you from a distance, he might get you confused with your sister, but not for long. Even though you're identical, there are subtle differences that I can see and I'm sure Balor will too."

"So you really think Brody will allow me to help fight this demon?" Kimi asked, clear apprehension in her voice.

"No, not unless things transpire differently than expected." Deacon pulled into the small parking lot at the airport and turned off the engine.

Silence followed as Lyn evaluated the conversation. "I don't get it. I don't understand any of this."

"They won't let her but there might not be a choice." Deacon turned his attention to Kimi. "I wouldn't let her fight."

"Do you think Brody is here?" Lyn changed the subject and dreaded the separation, remembering the last time they were apart and the ensuing havoc. Kimi was her voice of reason. Kimi helped her when she couldn't decide what way to go. Kimi kept her from finding trouble around the next bend. But she acknowledged that she'd changed since the incident with the Amazonian Devil. She'd lost some of that daredevil genetic makeup she'd once had. Now it was up to her to let Deacon play Kimi's role. The thought should unnerve her, but strangely it didn't.

25

"I will be with you in spirit, Lyn, and understand I don't like this any better than you do." Kimi stepped from the car and walking to the passenger side, gave Lyn a quick hug.

"I'll call when we get wherever it is we are going." Lyn swiped the tears from her cheeks, already missing her twin.

"No, you won't." Deacon held out his hand for Lyn to take. "Can't risk a trace on the call. I will stay in contact with Brody and he'll let you know whatever he feels you can handle."

"It's about time the three of you got here." Brody and Carr strode from the small terminal to meet the trio.

So, Carr was driving the Ferrari to Cactus Junction. Lyn had wondered what would happen to the car and what was appearing to be Deacon's modus operandi; he had a plan for everything. When and where were they teleporting, unless Deacon too, had a plane at his disposal?

"Is the jet ready?" Kimi gave Brody a hug and Lyn followed suit.

With hands in his pockets, Brody rocked back on the heels of his boots and sent Lyn a wink. "Yup."

"Is there food?" Kimi asked.

"Yup."

"Good, because I'm starving." Kimi walked toward the terminal, turning at the door to wave to her sister. "Good luck. I'll do everything I can to get to you."

"Thanks," Lyn's heart sunk, knowing that task would be daunting, but she still prayed Kimi would find a way.

It wasn't like her family to abandon anyone yet here they were, leaving in two different directions. She had to believe Brody and Carr thought it best, but she couldn't help the misgivings racking her brain.

Carr wrapped an arm around her shoulders. "Everything will turn out for the best. Deacon, here has his family with him and Brody and I will join you soon."

"Then you know where Deacon is taking me?"

"Not yet, but we'll find out shortly. Trust him, Lyn. He won't fail you." Carr bent down and gave her a quick kiss on the cheek. "Go on now."

Christine Young

Lyn didn't want to leave Carr's arms. With his thumb, Carr wiped a tear from her cheek. "I'm afraid."

"Don't be. Remember to use your head and not your heart. Think before you act or react. I'll see you in a couple of days." With that said, Lyn watched as Deacon handed Carr the keys to the Ferrari.

In a few seconds it roared to life and Carr was gone. Looking at Deacon now, "What happens next?"

"We go for a short walk and then..."

"Let me guess, we teleport."

"Yes..." He looked serious and very concerned. "Do you think you can handle the sensations again so soon?"

"I don't think I have a choice." Lyn rubbed her hands together, hoping the nausea wouldn't impact her as much as it had the last time.

"Don't suppose you do. I wouldn't do this if it wasn't necessary." Deacon took her hand in his and together they walked to a secluded corner outside the terminal.

Deacon inhaled a few long and deep breaths then peered around the corner for a second.

"I'm ready." Lyn wanted to get this over with. Exhaustion had begun to seep through every inch of her body. All she wanted right now was to sleep for twelve hours.

"That's my Sugar," Deacon said with an easy smile.

God, but his grin was sexy and sweet at the same time. His seeming ease in the face of this danger gave her confidence and helped her relax. She didn't know what to say.

He motioned for her. "Come here. Wrap your arms and legs around me then hold on tight. Whatever you do, don't let go."

Lyn followed his directions and leaning her head against his chest, listening to his slow even heartbeat. She closed her eyes and let the world spin around her for the second time that day.

~ * ~

Deacon slowed his heart rate and held Lyn as close as he could. In his arms, she felt small and fragile. He knew she was able to take care of herself better than most females, but she was also more important to him than any other woman he knew or would know. Closing his eyes, he set the events in motion, slowly at first then faster until the world spun and his body shook with the motion.

His world was about to implode. He prayed Brody and Carr would be able to kill Balor before the demon could find Lyn. It wasn't that he was afraid of a fight. Fuck. Adrenalin pumped faster through his body at the thought of killing the God of Death, but he understood the danger to Lyn. He was her last defense against Baylor. If he and her brothers went down, Lyn would be the sacrifice to the Fomori.

He inhaled a deep cleansing breath as the teleport came to an end.

The ground beneath his feet felt good; the trip to Nafplio quicker than he'd expected. But he'd never traveled this far with a beautiful vibrant woman in his arms and now he didn't want to let go of her. If he could pull her inside his heart and never let go, he would.

Deacon held on to Lyn longer than he needed to, soothing her by rubbing her back and neck with his hand. Putting his finger beneath her chin, he lifted and looked into her eyes. "You all right?" Concern for her ripped him apart. Her pale face and moisture-laden eyes sent guilt slithering within.

She licked her lips, nodding as her gaze met his. "Yes, I think so. Where are we?"

"Greece, a small town inland a few hours from Athens. It's located on a bay. I wish we were here under different circumstances."

Lyn turned in his arms to look around her, but there was nothing to see except walls. "Can I sit down? I'm feeling a little..."

"Of course." Deacon scooped her into his arms and walked around the building then down a long trail toward a town.

He stopped at a table and set her down on a pillowed chair beneath an umbrella. Sun shone and clouds flittered across the blue sky. People chatted in a foreign language around them. A soft breeze blew.

When a waiter stopped by their table, he ordered them both a cold drink. "You speak Greek?"

"Enough..." he grinned. "That's why I brought you here. There are lots of tourists so we won't stand out and most of the business folk speak English. You won't have trouble communicating."

"Do we have a place to stay?" She swiped hair from her face then swiveled in her chair as if to get a three hundred sixty degree view of the village.

"I've rented a small condo behind us."

He hoped she'd like the room, making sure there were two bedrooms and a pullout in the living room, for her emotional comfort. He needed her to trust then fall in love with him. Good lord, but he was already in love with her, and he didn't understand.

"For tourists?"

"Yes, but we have a small kitchen and two bedrooms and a living room." Her excitement gave him a reason to smile. Perhaps she could forget there was a demon after her.

The drinks arrived. "Can we get something to eat? I'm starving."

He laughed when her stomach used that moment to rumble. Then he turned serious, he hadn't thought of that. Of course, he was hungry too and she didn't have a dime. "Sorry, of course we can eat. What would you like?"

Lyn looked at the menu for a few minutes, then smiled at him. "Pick something for me."

"I can tell you what everything is." Then to the waiter, "Come back in a few minutes."

After a lesson of Greek menu one-o-one, Lyn was ready to order. Chicken Souvlaki, fried zucchini, French fries and tzatziki sauce. Deacon ordered Greek salad. They shared the food and when they finished, they walked through the small tourist town. Surrounded by water, a small fort sat in the middle of the bay.

They walked a while longer, the sun setting behind the fortress on the hill. To Deacon the scene was idyllic. He wished they were visiting under different circumstances. He could think of a dozen places he'd like to take her and a million things he'd like to do. There were so many beautiful sites within driving distance. He wanted to watch the sun set on the ocean by the Temple of Poseidon and so much more.

"Don't you get tired?" Lyn had stopped, staring at him as he was an anomaly.

"I'm sorry. I was enjoying the scenery and the company." He turned her and touched her cheek with the back of his hand, feeling protective. "When we finish here, I'll take you home."

"Home?" she queried, cocking her head with a sly smile on her lips.

"For lack of a better term, home for our duration here."

He wrapped an arm around her shoulders and led her toward town and up a narrow walkway to the condo he'd rented.

Inside, he turned on the lights and showed her around. Opening the door to the largest bedroom, "This is your room. I hope you find it comfortable."

He looked wistfully at the large king sized bed, wishing their relationship was at a point where they could share the warmth and comfort. Inside, he chided himself and gave himself reminders about not rushing her.

"Thank you. I don't suppose you thought about clothing?" She made a funny face and plopped down on the bed. "My bag, I assume is still in the hotel in Vegas."

"I did." He opened the closet door, showing her a dress and a shirt. In the dresser there was underwear and pajamas. "I guessed on the size. Tomorrow I'll take you shopping and you can buy whatever you want."

"I'll pay you back. This feels so comfortable. I feel as if I could sleep for twenty-four hours, but I won't."

"That won't be necessary. All the inconvenience of this is not your fault."

"Of course it will be and it's not your fault either."

"I'll let you go now. You have your own bathroom," he nodded toward a closed door. "Get some sleep and I'll see you in the morning." He kissed her forehead, wishing he had the nerve to kiss her on the lips, but he was a patient man and he knew waiting for the right time would be in his best interest.

"Good night," she said. "And you're sure we'll be safe here?"

Her question bit at his heart. Her safety was his first concern, and he hated that she had to ask. "For now." He closed the door to her room and strode into the living room, pulling his cell phone from his pocket as he walked. Texting Brody's number, he sat down on the sofa.

"We arrived safely and Lyn has gone to bed. Let me know if you have any sightings of Balor in or around Cactus Junction." His text went on longer than usual but there was a lot he needed to know.

When he finished, he set the phone down and waited for a reply. It would be early morning in Cactus Junction but he'd bet Brody was awake, the stakes in this game too high to take chances.

A few seconds later the reply came through. "We arrived safely. Kimi is asking too many questions I'm unable to answer at the moment. No sightings, but my gut tells me he's going to look here first."

"Yeah, you got everything handled on your end?" Deacon texted back, wishing their plans had been different. He fisted his hands, itching for a fight but knowing if the battle came here, Lyn would be involved and he'd do everything in his power to stop that from happening.

"The trap's in place. I just hope he falls for it and you can bring Lyn home before the week ends."

"Back at yah."

Lyn's home would be with him forever, if he had any say in this matter. She belonged to him. Convincing her might be harder than he thought. He'd been sure she'd recognize him as the man in her dreams, but she hadn't said anything. Needing to know where he stood with her was important, but not as much as her life.

When she'd been hurt, he hadn't known why he was there, watching her, holding her hand, encouraging her to live. But now he understood the ramifications and he'd hoped she would figure it out. Even if she did decipher the meanings, it wouldn't mean she was in love with him. Fuck, he didn't know how that felt, protective, eager to please, loving her wit and imagination, wanting her beside him forever. Was that love?

He leaned back on the couch, gazing outside. Stars twinkled and the moonlight filtered through the sliding glass doors leading to the deck. Closing his eyes, he tried to relax; afraid to fall asleep yet knowing he had to sleep sometime. Now seemed better than later. It would take some doing on Balor's part to locate them and Deacon felt sure the demon would look to her home in Cactus Junction first, then his in Northern California.

The scent of lilacs teased his senses. He opened his eyes to the sight of a sleepy-eyed Lyn walking past him to the little kitchenette. The short nightshirt left her long legs bare to his view. *Too fuckin' beautiful...*

When she reached high to grab a glass, he inhaled a swift breath of air and gripped the armrests. His body tensed. Then she bent over to scoop ice cubes and put them into his glass. His cock jumped to life. He closed his eyes, wishing she'd glide to the couch and sit down on his lap. Imagining how her naked body would feel next to his, her breasts against his chest, her lips melded to his. With only the tiniest leap, he imagined her breasts in his hands, the feel of her slick wet core.

When he opened his eyes, she'd vanished into her room. He heard the soft snick of her door closing. Swallowing hard, he willed his body to relax but the effort didn't work.

Seconds seemed to tick by like hours. The horizon grew lighter the birds began to chirp outside. He felt as if sand clouded his eyes, but the exhaustion he felt could not be channeled to sleep.

He sensed Lyn beside him before he saw her. He opened his eyes, sitting up and stretching.

"Can't you sleep?" Her query was bedroom soft and enticed his imagination further than he wanted it to go.

"No." *Not with you parading around in next to nothing.*

"I can't either. When I shut my eyes, my body keeps spinning. I feel as if only part of me made it here and the rest is trying to catch up. Everything, all my internal body clocks, seem messed up."

"I understand. I wish we could have taken our time, but we didn't have that elusive commodity."

She touched her hand on his arm. "It's not your fault. You only did what you thought necessary to protect me."

The way Lyn gazed at him made him more uncomfortable than he'd felt at his reaction to the sight of her nakedness. Now when she looked at him, he felt sure she looked into his soul. He didn't want to feel lacking, but somehow he did. He should have been able to make her feel so comfortable she wouldn't have trouble with sleep.

Reaching out to touch her cheek, he smiled, wishing he could go with her. "You should go back to bed."

Shrugging, "I won't be able to sleep. Is there anything we can do to speed this thing up? I don't want to run and hide the rest of my life. I'd like to encounter this demon and vanquish him."

"You're so sure the end result would be his death and not yours?" Deacon hated putting fear or doubt in her head, but she had to be realistic and patient in this endeavor.

"In the last two years we've killed two demons. I don't know why Balor would give us any more trouble than Jokul or the Amazonian Devil."

"The worst thing in this type of situation is over confidence. Your brothers and I are not waiting, running, or hiding. Brody is planning a trap and without any problems, they will end the demon in the next few days and you can return home."

Lyn pulled a pillow from the couch and snuggled it against her stomach. "What will you do then?"

Her innocent question stopped his breath. She must guess at their relationship at their destiny. "I will go with you."

"Ah," she nodded, scrunching up her nose as she grinned at him. "I know we're going to teleport there."

"Only if you want to. I thought we'd take a plane."

She frowned. "Not as fast. I think I'm getting used to lightning speed travel."

A creak of a floorboard outside the door caught Deacon's attention and set his heart racing. "Stay here."

~ * ~

The rutted out road Balor drove on jarred his nerves and rattled every bone in his body. He pulled to the side before opening his map; lines going everywhere made him grit his teeth with frustration. All the roads through this backwoods place seemed to be interwoven into what looked like a spider's web. He looked to the sky but it was still too dark for the sun to rise. East, west, what the hell direction was he traveling?

Feeling as if he'd been driving in circles, Balor leaned back on the seat, closing his eyes in hopes his raging headache would cease. He now had irrefutable evidence that he was lost...

...and hungry.

He'd never felt so alone in life or death.

The whiskey bottle was empty and he'd eaten all the candy and cookies he'd stolen. Once again, his stomach rumbled in protest. He reached into his pockets and found some coins and a few pieces of paper he'd learned could be exchanged for goods, but there was no store in sight, only rough roads and wilderness. If he had a knife or a bow, he could hunt game, but, alas, he had none of these items.

With nothing to do, save drive, he sat up and pushing on the gas pedal, followed the road, bouncing on each rut, his belly jiggling. If nothing else, it would lead him somewhere.

Hours later the sun had peaked its head above the tall fir trees, telling him he was driving the wrong way, north instead of south. He didn't know if he should turn around and go back the way he'd come or keep driving. The gas tank was one quarter full, and he knew if he turned around, he wouldn't find fuel before the car was empty.

Stopping the jeep, he let his head fall on the wheel. Tense seconds passed while he endeavored to think of another way. He could always try to find a different sacrifice, someone easier than Lyn McKenna who seemed to be protected by every shapeshifter in the world.

But he'd tried that ploy and failed.

No, the Fomori would send him back if he didn't bring Lyonesse McKenna. They would always send him back or they would kill him. Hell, he'd thought life would be fun, but resurrection hadn't played out the way he'd thought it would. He was miserable, dirty, hungry, exhausted and the list continued into eternity.

Heaving a long sigh, he looked up and gunned the engine. Maybe he'd find a gas station around the next bend.

The forest stretched on, slowly turning to rolling hills sprinkled with a few trees, but no gas, town, or market. His jeep chugged and shuddered to a rough stop. Swearing, Balor jumped from the car then kicked the tire, kicked it again and again, wishing the piece of rubber was the damn Fomori. He gave it one last kick before walking down the road. The sun might have just been rising when he was in the forest, but now it beat down on him, hot. Sweat trickled down his forehead and neck. With his sleeve, he wiped the moisture away and looked for a shady spot.

Spying one about twenty yards away, he started up a steep embankment intending to rest and cool off. Beneath his feet, dirt slipped and he found himself on all fours, trying to make the climb to shade. By the time he reached the top, sweat pooled beneath his pits and the back of his shirt was wet. He swiped at the moisture with his forearm.

He sat down, one hand over his heart, listening to the rapid and erratic cadence. He couldn't keep going like this. Shit, but when he caught up to that girl, he'd make her pay, exact his dues before he gave her to the sea demons for a sacrifice. The McKennas had put him through hell.

The hills seemed to roll in endless waves, the trees fuzzy and swirling. His gut twisted in a knot while the world spun around him. A sensation of falling consumed him as a dark tunnel encapsulated his trembling body.

Then he tumbled through time and space, seeing lights flash by at a lightning's pace. He landed hard, spraying water through the air before he was sucked into the darkness once more. Freezing liquid poured through his body.

He floated in water, his body still and his mind reaching out to the monsters of the deep.

What do you want?

You know.

I'm trying, but she has help. I didn't get to her soon enough. You sent me on a fool's mission. The McKennas have her.

It's the McClain who holds her.

Where?

We don't know, but you will find her. Your duty will be finished with us once we have her. Don't fail.

Failing was not part of his plan.

Release me and I will track her. I've not given up.

Desperate and exhausted, his body thrumming with pain, he was tossed from the sea and once more spun through the universe. He prayed they would find somewhere to put him that he could find food and another means of transportation.

When the twirling stopped, he found himself in the backseat of the jeep. His heart sped and the freezing sensation was replaced with the heat of the sun. Once again sweat beaded on his forehead. He leaned out the window and vomited on the dry ground beside the car.

He stayed in the car, staring at the ceiling, listening to the searing heat beat on the ground. Slowly, after thousands of seconds, a slight breeze filtered through the open window and night sounds echoed across the hills. His gaze darted through the vehicle, searching, looking for what he didn't know. Any second now, he expected to be tossed through the world again.

He wanted to stay here forever, but his stomach rumbled hungrily. Almost twenty-four hours had passed since he'd eaten the candy and cookies he'd stolen from the grocery store.

They could have sent a can of gasoline, but no...

Somewhere beyond the hills he could see and hear a coyote howling, sending shivers down his spine and following that, he heard the screech of a cat. That sent him over the backseat and ready to drive. Without thinking, he turned on the ignition and the car roared to life. He gunned the engine and sent dust billowing behind him as he raced down the road. The gas gauge read full.

He didn't care why he had gas now and could only surmise, but he wasn't going to spend time thinking about it. He hoped he'd reach a small town before he ran out again. A cat loped behind the vehicle. He stepped down on the accelerator and still the cat followed, but now the largest wolf he'd ever seen joined the cat.

Then another cat and another.

Adrenalin raced through him.

Chapter Three

After Deacon stepped outside, she decided to take a shower, wondering what it was Deacon would find in hallway. Certainly not Balor; probably a tourist. She turned on the water and walked inside after stripping. The water was deliciously hot.

Stepping from the shower, she towel dried and dressed before looking at herself in the mirror. She pulled her shirt tight and turned to the side, looking at her image then turning the other way. She leaned in close and smiled before making a face and sticking out her tongue. Good God, but she'd done everything she could think of to interest the man, but he'd not even blinked. Inhaling a deep breath, she tried to prepare herself for what was to come.

Maybe he wasn't the person she'd seen in her dreams. It had been over a year ago yet she felt his presence, understood the unmistakable draw to him. He didn't seem to get the connection though. Looking at herself in the mirror once more, she grimaced.

Too curvy, too leggy, too much on her hips. "Maybe he just doesn't like the way I look." Well then she couldn't be drawn to him because that way of thinking was superficial and shallow. Her soul mate would be someone who looked inside the person.

Well, she'd always had issues with her weight, anorexia had plagued her more than once and when she was sixteen she'd ended up in the hospital. She didn't know why she'd seen herself as fat, but after hours of counseling, she felt she'd conquered the disease. Kimi had stood by her throughout her hospitalization and recovery, stood by her now.

From what her brothers had told her about soul mates, it was all they could do to keep their hands off each other. And from the way Deacon responded to her, he didn't care to touch her at all, even to hold her hand.

So, she concluded, "we aren't soul mates." Visions of her overweight body swept through her head. She smoothed her hand down her stomach and reminded herself she wasn't fat.

I'm not fat. I'm just right.

Inhaling a huge breath of air and sighing with a dramatic flare, Lyn sat down on her bed then flung her body back, arms extended outward. She stared at the sterile white ceiling, would have counted lines if there had been any. She couldn't sleep, wasn't hungry, and couldn't think of anything that sounded appealing. Feeling as if she ached from the tips of her toes to her head could be a good explanation for what she was feeling.

Soft padding footsteps sounded through the thin walls of the apartment. Back and forth with a slow measured tread. The cadence of the steps was soft and soothing. Liking the sound, she smiled.

Deacon?

From the cadence she heard, she knew he wasn't sleeping either. He seemed to carry this protection thing to a degree beyond how her brothers treated her. She needed to show him she could take care of herself, defend against intruders. Strong and self-sufficient she'd never cringed or avoided a fight.

That's how I nearly died fighting the Amazonian Devil.

She had put up with Deacon McClain because he hadn't given her a choice. Manhandling her had been his only option. He didn't tell her why he was protecting her and from whom. If he wasn't her soul mate, what was his agenda?

It was time for him to tell her everything.

Her fingers resting on the doorknob, she paused and for one of the first times in her life, gave thought to her actions. With a slow shaking hand, Lyn turned the knob and peered out the tiny crack. No one came into view, but she could still hear the tread of soft feet. Pushing the door a little wider the scene encompassing more of the room, her heart lurched and she inhaled a swift hiss of air.

The white tiger stalking the room stopped, his gaze riveted on her, seeming to pierce her soul. Lyn stepped back and shut the door tight. Leaning against the wood, her hand on her chest, she tried to breathe but her lungs seemed sealed shut even while her heart pounded a rapid staccato.

In her heart she'd known he was a shifter, but now she'd seen first hand and he was magnificent, so beautiful.

Perfect.

Swallowing hard, she stepped from the door and opened it again, her gaze sweeping the room. She'd wanted to see him in his cat form, but she'd waited too long. Deacon was standing, his back to the door, pulling on his jeans. His waist was narrow and as her gaze traveled upward she saw a well-muscled back. When he turned, the sight of him stole her breath again.

"You should be in bed. I know you're tired," He told her as he slipped a t-shirt over his head and pulled it down. His gaze once again riveted on her, seemed to delve inside.

Her hand at her throat, "So should you," she countered, wanting to stay up until she found out who the real Deacon McClain was. He hadn't even touched on that bit of information. She knew so little about him.

He shrugged. "Couldn't, too much to think about. I'm worried."

"What did you find in the hallway?"

"Nothing, a maid."

"At this time of night?"

"Yes, I suppose it is a bit strange, but I'm convinced she was telling the truth."

Lyn sat down and curling her legs beneath her she stared at Deacon for a few more seconds. "Okay, let's forget about the maid. I think there is an awful lot you need to tell me. I'm not known for my patience and I'm almost to the end of my limits. Neither of us can sleep so what better time for you to talk? I'd like to understand what I'm facing. And," she paused. "I want to know all about you, what you're not telling me."

Sitting down opposite Lyn, Deacon took her hand in his. His callouses told her he was a workingman and he didn't spend his time sitting behind a desk. She liked his touch and the corresponding thoughts. To learn as much as she could about this man was paramount.

"I don't know where to start." His smile was half-hearted. For a few seconds he looked away, gazing out the window before he turned back to face her.

The need to understand him was important. "At the beginning is usually the best." She ran her thumb across the top of his hand. What was it about him? She trusted him unconditionally even though all her training spoke to the contrary. Her brother's words to be wary echoed through her head.

Don't trust anyone...

"I'm not sure what that is...the beginning." The slanted smile and focused eyes sent her mind in a tailspin. "There is so much I don't know either. Some of the facts I've pieced together, some I'm assuming are facts."

"What or who am I running from? And don't mince words." Her challenge came from deep-seated emotions; the McKennas did not keep secrets. "I have the right to know."

He let go of her hand, rising to pad around the room before speaking. "Balor, he's a Celtic demon, known as Balor of the evil eye. When he was a child, his curiosity got the best of him, and he entered a room forbidden to him. His father's druids were boiling an evil potion in a cauldron. As the brew began to bubble, drops spattered into his eye. Because of this he has the ability to bring fear and havoc to any who look into it. Some say looking into his eye is deadly." He continued the story while Lyn nodded and tried hard to understand what this Balor guy had to do with her.

"So if I look in his eye, I'll die," she stated. Thinking about the morbid fact did little to erase her confusion or relieve her shredded nerves.

"Probably not. It doesn't seem to have the same effect on shifters. Anyway, Balor was the Lord of Tory Island off the western coast of Ireland. He had a beautiful daughter but because of a prophecy that a grandchild of his would kill him, he kept her locked in a room on the island."

"That's horrible. I can't imagine my father locking me in a room surrounded by water. Although there were several times in my teen years he threatened to do something like that." With growing interest in Deacon's story, Lyn listened attentively, still wondering what all of this had to do with her and why Deacon had resorted to teleportation to whisk her away from her family and her home.

"As the legend goes, a young man by the name of Cian swam to the island and found his way into her room. He slept with her and as a result she became pregnant with triplets."

"That's amazing, triplets. Are you making this up?" she asked, tempted to laugh but still too curious to stop the flow of words from her would-be rescuer.

"Not at all, it's a story that's been handed down through generations. I made a point to find out more when I learned Balor was on a quest to find you."

"Why me, would you have done the same thing if he'd been after Kimi?"

He sighed, seeming to wince at the question but didn't hesitate with his answer. "Yes, I would have because she is your sister, your family. Anyone who is important to you deserves my protection when in trouble."

"That was the right answer, but I still don't understand your connection to my family. I'll figure it out in time though. Now tell me more about Balor."

"Well, Balor was furious when he learned about the babies. The last thing he'd wanted was grandchildren, knowing one was fated to kill him. Her father was so furious that his daughter feared for their lives. She put the infants into a boat to save them but two of them drowned. The surviving child was known as Lugh Llamhfada."

"If Balor is alive, Lugh didn't kill him."

"Lugh killed him, but the Fomori brought him back to life for the sole purpose of providing sacrificial maidens for them."

Realization dawned as she felt blood drain from her face. Her mind spinning, she clutched at the pillow she held in front of her, trying to calm the ragging nerves sweeping inside. "They want me as a sacrificial virgin? Who the hell are the Fomori? And what if we told them I'm not a virgin?"

His brows drew together at her words and he shifted in his chair. "I won't let that happen. But he's very powerful, yet not very smart it seems. The Fomori are demons who rule the seas in Ireland and the surrounding area. They've decided they want Lyn McKenna for the next sacrifice and sent Balor to find you and bring you to them."

"Geez, have you had contact with him? With Balor?" She had wanted to hear this and now she wished she hadn't. How many demons were there in this world and would they ever leave her family alone?

"I've had some interaction with the demon. Obviously, Balor was the man I fought in the casino."

"And that's why you wanted me out of there fast. I barely had time to breathe and you whisked me away. Now I'm in Greece and waiting for him to find me. Why don't we join with my brothers and find him first?" Sitting and waiting wasn't her style. Attack, take the offense, seemed the best way to act, but on the other hand, she wasn't about to do something stupid that would put her in the hands of Balor. Becoming a sacrifice to sea demons was not part of her future plans and she did want to have a future.

"We, Brody and I, believe he will go to Cactus Junction. Your brothers are waiting for him and hope to deal with him before he can find you."

"Yeah, you've said that before, and I don't like it any better this time than I did the last." Lyn walked to the window. She still wasn't sleepy, just exhausted and hungry. The sun was rising over the bay. An urge to run and release tension filled her. Putting her hands on the small of her back, she stretched and waited for Deacon to say something.

Deacon joined her by the window, one hand on her shoulder and massaged the kinks. "What would you like to do? Sleep? Eat?"

She shrugged his hand off, not wanting to feel weak even though she enjoyed the small gesture of intimacy. "Run. I want to go for a run in the forest. I want to feel free and without a care if only for a short time."

"Cat or human form? This is the off season, so I think we could find somewhere empty of people to shift."

"A swim and a run?" Lyn was hopeful the answer would be yes.

"I think I know the perfect place, but I'd like food first."

"Fine, I could use coffee and a bite of something." Walking into her bedroom, she paused at the dresser then rummaged through the few items she'd bought the day before. "I don't have a swimsuit."

Deacon turned and grinned. "Skinny dipping works for me."

Not finding anything, Lyn turned and tossed a pillow at him. "We can swim as cats."

"I think I'd like that." Deacon leaned on the windowsill, gazing over the scene below. "How long will it take you to get ready?"

"Ten minutes tops. I'll race you." She searched the dresser for appropriate clothing.

"I'm ready now."

"Give me five. I just want to brush my teeth." Lighthearted for the first time since she'd first encountered Deacon, she raced into the bathroom, emerging a few minutes later in a pair of shorts and a halter-top.

Deacon stepped forward and took her hand in his. "It would be best if we pretended to be a couple."

Lyn cocked her head to one side, trying to gauge his thoughts. *Pretend?* "What are you up to?"

"Just want to make sure we aren't conspicuous. This is one of the most romantic cities in the Peloponnese. According to mythology, this town was founded by Nafplios, the son of Poseidon and the daughter of Danaus Anymone. Do you want to know more?"

"Yes, it is interesting but not right now. Let's go." She led the way to the door, eager for the run and swim.

Deacon locked the door behind them and strode to the front lobby with his hand linked to Lyn's. A few people dotted the streets. They stopped at a small outdoor café, ordering coffee and bread with cucumbers and tomatoes.

The skies were a brilliant blue color with a few low lying clouds dotting the horizon, and the temperature was perfect, warm enough for a swim but not too hot for a run.

An hour later, the couple was strolling along a path near a beach. Water lapped on the sand and sunrays turned the water to silver ripples.

"Run first?" Deacon asked.

"Of course." She winked and slanted him what she hoped was a sexy-wicked smile.

They separated to find private places to shift. Lyn stood behind a rock, forest behind her.

Disrobing, she folded each piece of clothing, leaving a neat pile then closed her eyes and let energy flow within. Her body quivered and heated with renewed life. She felt the change from the tips of her toes to her head and suddenly she stood on all four feet. She grinned, loving the feelings sweeping through her. When she turned, she saw Deacon standing in his human form in front of her.

She cocked her head to the side and watched his easy grin. Then swishing her tail, she waited.

"I like your new look, Sugar."

Why hadn't he changed? She sat back on her haunches and stared at him as he winked at her then slowly stripped. He didn't say another word, but their gazes were locked and she thought she heard him purring. Good Lord, he was gorgeous. He didn't turn around when he slipped from his jeans.

She was sure she was drooling. Her heart pounded and she thought every nerve ending had snapped.

He was such a tease.

She'd never watched anyone shift before. Her brothers certainly didn't let her watch and for some reason she'd never seen Kimi change forms. Yet it seemed so right—so perfect and intimate to watch Deacon now.

When he finished, he padded over to her. His tail twitching, he moved his head toward the path, seeming to indicate she was to lead the way and he would follow. High on speed but not much on endurance, she started slow but within a few minutes she picked up the pace, reveling in the sensations. Wind beat against her face and her paws pounded against the ground. The earth flew past.

When she turned her head to make sure he followed, Deacon seemed to hold back. He was so much larger and probably more powerful. With no warning, he stopped looking at her, an easy walk, then a lope, and before she could blink, he was beside her, his power and speed all-encompassing. They ran through the countryside, along animal paths. Trees, shrubs, flowers all passed by in a blur. Then they hit the beach, the sand softer than the dirt trails.

He ran alongside her then turned her toward the bay. Winded, she was ready for a rest but knew she would keep up with him as long as she could. She didn't want to him to think she couldn't keep pace. Sometimes Kimi chided her for being too competitive, but this time Kimi would urge her to run beside him. It seemed as if they were one.

Stopping on the sandy beach, Lyn inhaled a long deep breath of air. Her lungs burned from the run, her legs sore and her heart raced. She felt fulfilled and vibrant. She'd been inactive too long and knew she needed to shift and run in her cat form more often. Trips to the gym had been too few and far apart. Runs in her cat form in the Sierra Madres were becoming increasingly more dangerous with outward spread of civilization.

Deacon sat beside her, but gazed outward. He too seemed to be recovering from the run and that made her feel better. There was her competitive monster coming to the forefront again.

Taking the lead, she rose and padded into the sea. There she let the gentle swells wash over her until she had to swim. He was beside her, long sure strokes propelled him forward yet she knew he held back. Speed wasn't everything. With her tongue, she lapped the salty water once then stopped, knowing she couldn't risk dehydration.

But she was tired, exhausted from the turmoil of the last twenty-four hours and sure she'd exercised enough to sleep. She caught his attention and motioned to turn back.

A few minutes later they'd headed for land. A scent on the breeze sent her nerves crashing to a panicked halt. Instinctively, she knew danger was close. Deacon seemed to sense the peril too, moving closer to her.

He turned her so they headed for a spit of land at least a half-mile away. She inhaled deep breath of air and was rewarded with salt water. Every muscle in her body cried out in pain, but she made herself swim. Stopping now wasn't an option.

Hours seemed to pass before they reached land. Lyn crawled onto sand and let her head fall against her paws. Deacon paced in a circle around her, stopping every few seconds to nudge her face with his chin. Exhausted, she couldn't move, but she sensed safety here, where Deacon had taken her.

He lay down beside her and she closed her eyes, relishing the catnap he was allowing her. If he'd asked, she couldn't have moved. The morning had started out wonderfully...

~ * ~

...how would it end?

In so many ways the ending to this was up to her. Forest lay beyond, safety, a hiding place, but she had to shake herself from her self-imposed depression and walk to safety. Where was the twin who took on the Amazonian Devil? Shivering in her boots?

For another few seconds she closed her eyes and tried to breathe in deep breaths of air. Calming her racing heart, she rose and looked at Deacon, giving him her approval to go, to move forward, digging deep for courage.

Deacon worried about her. She looked so tired, exhausted. He didn't know how to fix this. An enemy was close but it wasn't Balor. He could smell Balor. The scent of fish and seawater was not on the wind. This scent, pure evil, permeated every space.

What was it?

Humans?

Perhaps, but this didn't seem quite right. If he could walk the distance to the trees and protection for Lyn, he would. If he could carry her on his back, he would. All he could think to do was to nudge her forward. It had been a ridiculous idea to run today. He should have insisted she sleep.

But sleep had been elusive for him and he expected the same for her. Regrets pummeled through him. Hunger rumbled in his belly, but he didn't hear anything from Lyn. She was so tired, hunger was no longer an emotion for her. Against his wishes, he urged her to stand and nodding toward the safety of shelter, he urged her forward.

Padding across sand then soft dirt littered with leaves, they reached the line of trees and he found a place for her to lie down. Standing guard against an unknown enemy while she slept was paramount.

He just didn't understand. Nafplio was supposed to be safe. No one knew they had gone to Greece let alone this little known resort town. So what was happening?

Reaching a forested shelter, Lyn curled into a tight ball, falling asleep almost as soon as she shut her eyes. He listened to her deep breathing, wishing he hadn't pushed her so hard, but he'd wanted to understand her limits. Needed to know what she was capable of enduring and what she wasn't. He'd never expected danger so soon and so close.

He was an idiot and he chided himself for this stupidity as he paced the perimeter he'd set up around Lyn.

The sun was high in the sky. The noon hour had just passed. He would let her sleep until dusk. Returning under dark would be for the best. He lay down beside her, refusing to shut his eyes, knowing it could result in death for both of them if he did.

Beside her, he felt her body quiver with fatigue and fear. Erasing those feeling overrode every other thought. She was his to take care of and at the moment he wasn't doing his job.

She moved her head so it rested on his legs. He wished he was in human form so he could pull her into his arms and comfort her with his body as well as his words. Now all he had were her thoughts.

The danger he'd felt had been strong and persistent, but he couldn't figure out who or what the threat was. Balor wasn't in Nafplio, his scent would linger on the air if he was any place close.

Christine Young

This new hazard perplexed him. Not knowing from what direction this unexpected peril would come made this job so much harder. He looked at his woman, asleep and already so dear to him.

She purred and nestled in closer to his side. He would have to wake her soon, would have to scour the perimeter before risking the swim back or the much longer trek around the bay. At the moment there were no strange scents on the breeze.

But that could change quickly. He suspected the danger had left the area, but that didn't mean he shouldn't be careful. Lyn stretched and rolled over, meeting his gaze. She blinked several times then stretched again. He wanted to tell her what was going on but didn't want to frighten her either.

Remembering the look in her eyes when she saw him naked just before he shifted, left an imprint in his head, one he couldn't shake. Her eyes had been wide, her mouth formed a small 'o', then she'd looked down.

Her reaction to him was not something he'd been able to read. Nonetheless, he was going to have to shift back and talk to her. Fig leaves had their appeal. He was in paradise and there might be a fig tree somewhere, but he couldn't see one nearby.

He tried to tell her with gestures to stay and she seemed to understand. Rising from his position, he strolled into the forest. The air was clear and fresh. Wood smells abounded, but nothing told him to fight or flee. As he made his way through the underbrush, he listened to the sounds.

Nothing significant or out of the ordinary...

The sensations began at his head, his body shaking with adrenalin and igniting the energy needed to change form. The experience wasn't new. He'd shifted hundreds of times, but this was different. Urgency filled every sinew of his body. Fear for Lyn drove his actions. Always before he'd felt carefree and easy.

In his human form now, he looked for something to wrap around his body or at least hold in front of his cock. What a conundrum. He wanted nothing more than to get down and dirty with Lyn, but not this way. With a shrug of his shoulders and a heavy intake of breath, he sauntered through the brush to stand butt naked in front of her.

She stared at him, eyes wide, and he cursed silently then he thought he saw her grin, but he couldn't be sure. He wanted to see inside her head, hear her thoughts.

He crouched down close to her. "I know you can understand what I say, so listen carefully."

She nodded; the grin fading. "Good girl, Sugar."

She barred her teeth. "I understand, but I'm not placating and I won't apologize for calling you Sugar."

She shook her head. "No, I don't want you to shift. I'm going to change back as soon as I tell you why we're here."

She stiffened, her tail twitching and her body showing all the stress of the last few hours.

"Back on the mainland, I caught the sent of danger. I don't know where it was coming from."

Her body tensed more and she started to rise. He placed his hand on her head and rubbed her ears. "It wasn't Balor."

Trustingly, she relaxed and leaned into his hand a soft purr emanating from her. It seemed she tried to tell him she was listening and understood.

"I don't know what it was. I'm going to scout the perimeter, planning to walk back instead of swim. We can stay in the shadows and even though the land route might take longer, I believe it will be safer. Are you up to it?"

She nodded and rose, her tail moving from side to side and waited.

"Not yet, Sugar. I want to take a look around. I'll be back in few minutes. Stay here and wait for me."

Her body arched before she settled down and set her head on her paws, eyes wide.

"Good." A moment's relief filled him. Her attitude was good and he felt sure she wouldn't act on impulse.

He made his way around the area and returned to see Lyn in the same spot, waiting.

"It's time and the area looks secure."

Quickly shifting to his cat form, Deacon led the way back to the little town from where they started their excursion this morning. The time he'd planned for her was supposed to have been relaxing and fun. He'd wanted to take her mind off the demon chasing her.

But the day had not turned out as he'd intended.

They walked and ran, then rested. The sun set and the moon rose over the hills, lending a small measure of light. Numerous times, Deacon turned back to make sure Lyn was following, ready to stop whenever necessary.

Hours later they found their clothes at the base of the rock where they'd left them. A few thoughts had arisen as they'd walked. He'd been worried the clothes might not be there and he'd have to figure out a way back to the condo without being seen.

But the clothes were waiting for them. He turned his back on Lyn to allow her time to change form and dress. Then he did the same. Hand in hand they strolled back to the town and found an outside café to eat.

"I'm starving." Lyn stared at the menu, running one finger over the entrées. "I think I could order everything on it and still not feel satisfied."

"Order as much as you want." Deacon grinned, loving watching her and relieved they were back and safe within the confines of the village.

"I have a feeling my eyes are bigger than my stomach, but I do want a glass of wine to start then I'll get the chicken and fried zucchini."

"I want a hamburger, but I'll order the same since they don't seem to have burgers on the menu."

"Not a fan of Greek food?"

"Love it. Just have a hankerin' for red meat and American venue. Chicken will have to do for now."

The waiter came to their table with the wine they'd ordered when they first sat down. "Tell me what happened back there. Everything seems to be a blur. I don't know why we ran, but instinct took over."

"That's the thing, I don't know. I can't get a handle on the fear or the strange scents emanating from the forest."

"Or your gut intuition. Brody always told me to trust the gut. It never lies." She sipped her wine, then swirled it around the glass. "But you don't think it's Baylor. So who wants to give me or us grief?"

"Even if I hadn't sensed something else, unless Baylor learned how to teleport, he couldn't have made it from California to Nafplio in less than twenty-four hours. A private jet maybe, but I really don't think..."

"Besides Athens, where is the nearest airport?"

"A private jet..."

Lyn pushed her hair away from her face then picked at the zucchini the waiter had just set in front of them. "You're right. He couldn't have reached here, besides didn't you think he'd try Cactus Junction and your home before he searched the rest of the world for me?"

"I did and I do. He doesn't know where we are. It's going to take him some time to find out, if he ever does."

"So we've come full circle. Who or what stirred your gut reaction to get me—us away from the area." She forked apiece of chicken before sticking it in her mouth and chewing with a puzzled expression.

He leaned back, rubbing his chin in thought. "I overheard someone. I caught some people talking about poachers in this area. But I didn't think..."

"Are there other shifters here?" Lyn asked; her eyes wide as her attention moved from her food to him.

"Could be and if there are, we might find help from them if the need arises." Deacon wasn't sure he wanted help from an unknown source. He'd always made it a point not to trust anyone and this situation was no different.

"If you're right and there are poachers, do you think they saw us? I know what poachers are capable of doing."

She looked too nonchalant, too uncaring of the danger. "They might have seen us or thought they caught a glimpse."

"Then we better not shift again. We were taking a pretty big risk as it was." Lyn's eyes narrowed as she cocked her head to one side as she twirled a piece of zucchini in the sauce.

"Agreed," he worked the chicken off the sticks and popped one into his mouth, gazing at her.

"First thing tomorrow, I'd like to shop. I really need some clothes and underwear."

Shit, but he'd been such a dunce, of course she needed thing; he did too. "First thing," he promised.

They finished and paid the check, then strolled down the boulevard toward the hotel. Stopping at a small grocery store, they picked up a few things for breakfast and a bottle of wine and popcorn for a late night snack.

The hallway in front of their door was empty. "I'll go in first." Deacon unlocked the door and stepped through, looking both ways as he entered. The light on a corner table was on, just as he'd left it, and the door to the main bedroom was open. He could see inside but he wanted to walk through it before he let Lyn come into the room.

"Anyone there?" she asked, moving toward the door.

"Give me a minute to look through the closets and the other rooms." He wished this wasn't necessary, but under the circumstances, it was.

"You've got to be kidding. The door was still locked. Who could be inside? I doubt the manager would give anyone a key."

"No Sugar, I'm not joking. I want to make sure everything is safe. Where you're concerned, I'm not taking any chances."

"All right..."

A few seconds later, "It's clear. Come on in." He set the groceries on the counter and proceeded to put them away, then uncorked the wine and poured them both a glass.

Lyn walked to the balcony and sat down, plopping her feet on a small table. "It's beautiful. I wish the day had turned out different. I don't like the feel that someone wants to hurt us."

"Me too." He handed her the wine before sitting down. The breeze was warm and refreshing giving thought to a pleasant evening. Sounds of tourists and natives, eating and laughing wafted upward.

"I miss Cactus Junction and my family. I want to go home and have everything normal again."

He watched her expression, wishing he could make all of this go away and hoping the next call from Brody McKenna would bring them home. "Tell me about them, your family; your roots."

She laughed and he liked the way her eyes lit up with whatever humorous thought had crossed her mind. "Well, my new found friend, you're in for a long night, and I don't know if I can stay awake. But I'll give you a brief introduction. Maybe when we can go to my home, I'll take you up to Infinity Cliff. The view is one of a kind."

"I'd like that." He leaned back, one arm draped across the back of his chair, trying to relax and think of pleasant thoughts. Yet with every pause, he remembered the scents of the day, recalled the fear and his gut reaction. He couldn't shake the fear he'd seen in Lyn's eyes from his mind.

"My Scottish ancestors live close to yours. Do you still live in Ireland?" She set the wine on the small glass table in front of her.

He shook his head. "No, I make my home in northern California, near Yosemite."

"I've never been to Yosemite," she changed the subject for a brief moment. "I've pretty much lived in Cactus Junction my entire life. My brothers have kept a pretty close guard over their younger siblings and Mom and Dad watch proprietarily over all of us. But in the long run, I think my parents gave Kimi and me a lot of room to discover and learn. Let us be curious and explore life. But then," she shrugged. "What could happen in the middle of the Sierra Madres?" she paused, "Not much."

A lot. "You forget the Amazonian Devil so quickly? And your fight to live?" He rose and leaned on the railing, remembering their first meeting. She'd been close to death and lying in the sweat lodge, and he'd been with her through her dreams. He'd never forget those terrifying days.

~ * ~

Kimi stretched out on a lawn chair behind her parent's home, loving the feel of the sunshine on her flesh as well as the warmth. The last half hour all she'd done was think about Lyn. Where she was and what was happening. Brody had told her a little about the demon and why he chased Lyn, but none of it made sense. Her parents had wanted to hunt Balor down and kill him, but Brody told them he had a better plan. As far as she could tell, her brother's plan consisted of waiting and watching then doing it all over again.

A water balloon hit her on the legs. She shrieked and jumped, knowing it was her little brother's handiwork, but was surprised to see Carr standing over her when she looked up.

"What the hell..." She wasn't angry. The water felt wonderful on her hot skin, but she wanted to retaliate, remembering many romps across the lawn with water weapons in hand.

"Time you got out of the sun. You burn too easily," Carr told her with an arrogant shrug of his broad shoulders. *There he goes again, playing the big brother.*

"I have sunscreen on." She felt a bit indignant at the accusation she couldn't take care of herself, but knew he meant well.

"Then why are you red?"

She looked at herself. "That's a tan."

"Guess I've got a different definition of tan. Brody has called a family meeting in ten minutes."

Family meeting? That must mean he's learned something or has actually planned something. They'd been at home for a few days now and there had been little to no mention of the danger, at least not when she was around.

"Where?"

"Dad's office." Carr walked off in another direction, presumably to spread the news.

A few minutes later, showered and dressed in shorts and t-shirt, she plopped down on an overstuffed chair in one corner of the room. She had a glass of ice tea in one hand and a stack of cheese and crackers in the other and was not surprised to find she was the first to arrive.

Munching on her snack, she watched the others file into the office. Next was Guy, the youngest brother, then Carr and Margo. Brody and Sadie walked in hand in hand, then Angel and Phaedra. The sight of the dark brooding man who shifted into the hugest wolf she'd ever seen, striding with Phaedra, the woman who had helped Margo escape the ice demon surprised her, but following them was someone she'd never seen before.

The McKennas were rallying the forces—all of them.

The one person missing was her great grandfather. He rarely came down from the secluded mountaintop he called home.

Last but carrying trays of drinks, her parents walked through the door. Brody stood in front of everyone assembled, arms crossed in front of him, feet planted firmly apart.

It was so 'take charge' Brody.

"I believe you all know why I called this meeting." He cleared his throat. "Please welcome Angel and Phaedra. They will stay with us until this is over and Lyn can return home. And," he paused, "this is a friend of Angel's, Maska O' Keefe. We call him Mak."

Kimi really didn't know what to think. The first sight of him left her breathless and lightheaded, and she didn't like that feeling. "Can Maska be trusted?"

All heads turned her way. She didn't know why she'd blurted out the question. She usually said nothing and did what she was told, but there was just something about this man, something familiar.

Something that had her second-guessing her intuition.

Brody looked at Angel. Angel nodded.

"Angel will vouch for him. His clan is familiar to Angel's and he has been of great service on a number of occasions." Brody rocked on the balls of his feet and looked to their father.

Mak stepped forward. "I know I must prove myself. Trust is earned, but I assure everyone I have the Clan Chatton's best interest in my heart. I was born of the Sioux nation, but lived in a remote spot in Ireland. I have come to the States to live and have taken up residence near Yosemite and close to Deacon McClain. He has befriended me and I would not like anything to happen to anyone he holds dear."

Maska stepped back, arms crossed in front of his chest before blending in with her family as if he belonged. His dark hair and brilliant blue eyes penetrated her soul. When she wanted to look away, she found herself staring at him and wanting to run her finger across his strong jawline and maybe more.

56

"I'm sure the question paramount on everyone's mind is 'where is Lyn?' But I'm not at liberty to divulge that secret. Instead, I ask for your patience. With time, you will all know. Hopefully we will destroy Balor and bring Lyn back without having to divulge her whereabouts."

"Why did you call the meeting?" Carr stepped forward, his expression grim. "Has anyone seen the demon?"

"Yes," Brody began.

"Where?" the group chorused and if the situation wasn't so dire, Kimi would have found it amusing. Instead she sipped on her tea and ate another cracker while trying to look at Mak from behind lowered eyelashes.

Brody laughed, "Sadly, he seems to be lost in the desert."

"You say that tongue in cheek?" Guy seemed to bristle with Brody's amusement.

"I'm just thinking of all the ways we can terrorize this sea demon who is lost on an ocean of sand." Brody looked pointedly at his siblings. "The sad part is that we will have to end him. There is no other way to keep our sister safe."

"You don't think the Fomori will send someone else to find her?" Carr's tone was sounded grim.

Brody shook his head. "No, I don't they will. Balor is paying his debt for regaining his life. The sea creatures will look for sacrifices closer to home. It seems they were tricked into bringing him back from the dead and have made his new life horrific."

"What do you have in mind?" Angel stepped forward. "I will do all that I can to help."

"We find him and terrorize him as he has frightened Lyn."

"And how do you plan on accomplishing that feat?" Guy asked from his corner of the office.

"We're all shifters. I propose we shift and find him in the desert. I'm sure all of our howls and screeches will make him speechless. With that accomplished, we kill him."

"Sounds simple enough," Carr said, "but we all know how plans can go awry. Do you have a backup plan?"

"I'm working on it."

Chapter Four

Lyn curled up on the couch, a second glass of red wine in hand and gazed out the windows toward the bay, her thoughts spinning a million different directions. Deacon sat down next to her, turned a bit sideways so he could watch her. She sipped the wine before reaching for a handful of popcorn.

"You going to tell me about your clan? If you're not ready, I can wait." He sat down beside her, beer in hand and a second bag of popcorn. "But I really don't want to—wait that is."

God, he was gorgeous in his tight shirt that accented every muscle. She reached out and touched his hand, enjoying the time with him even though danger seemed to come at them from every angle. What was in store for them? For her? What if this demon chasing her found her and killed Deacon? She couldn't stomach that idea.

"I've nothing to hide from you." For a moment she looked away unable to accept the thought that the danger surrounding them would win. In the end, she wanted to explore her feelings for this man and find out if he was her mate. That seemed so tacky to her but in her world that's exactly what the man she was meant to be with the rest of her life was called.

Her mate, her soul mate.

He took her hand in his, pulling her into his arms then resting his head on top of hers. A brief few seconds of quiet gave her peace. The warmth of his body next to hers made her feel protected and safe. She closed her eyes, thinking of the possibilities of poachers practically on their doorsteps and of

Balor thousands of miles away. The first danger seemed more real and menacing. How could they infiltrate this gang and end them? The irony didn't escape her.

He waited for her to talk with a sexy smile on his face, seeming too damn patient. He pushed her hair from her face and gently held it behind her head before letting loose ends fall around her cheeks.

"Well, where to start? There is so much to tell." She cleared her throat and let her head fall against his chest. "The McKenna Clan lived in Scotland, some still do. But then you already knew that. Tales have them living in the Highlands for millions of years, if that's possible."

"I did know. My clan infiltrated Ireland." He traced a calloused fingertip down her neck, stopping at her ear to trace the shell. Her body shuddered at the feel of his gentleness. "And I think we both understand that anything is possible. It's just that some stories are more believable than others. We all do what is necessary to survive."

The erotic touch sent shivers of heat down her spine and sent her body into spiraling emotions. Her history, his history, and they might blend together in the future to create their own story.

Anything was possible.

She licked her suddenly dry lips and swallowed hard to bring moisture to her parched throat. His hands framed her face and his gaze met hers, studying, looking into her eyes as if he could see into her soul. "We were and still are known as the clan Chattan."

"Clan of the cats," he parroted, and followed the path of his fingers with his lips, her ear, her neck. His light touch caressing every nerve ending, giving credence to the tenderness that seemed to be so much a part of this man.

"Yes," she trembled, wishing he would never stop, knowing she wasn't ready for intimacy. Not at this moment, yet understanding it was inevitable. She touched his jaw and traced the hard line to his ear before dropping her hand, afraid of her emotions.

Lyn lost her train of thought and turned into him, looking up. He kissed her then, a gentle kiss, one that spoke of promises to come…perhaps a life together. He touched her nose with his lips, followed the line of her eyebrows. "You have beautiful eyes; they are the color of a summer sky."

"Do you want to hear more?" She didn't know if she could talk and if he kept this up, she knew she'd melt into a mindless puddle right at his feet.

"Of course." He pulled back and grinned at her as if his touch did nothing to her-to him. "Tell me all about your clan-your family."

"Then you have to stop kissing me."

"Umm... don't know if I can do that." But he pulled back and gave her breathing room.

Deacon's arm still draped across her shoulder; she began to recount the story. "In 1831, eight members of the McKenna clan in Scotland left for the United States. They searched for large spaces and room to explore uncharted territory. That was almost two hundred years ago, but the story stays alive among the people."

"The McClains did much the same. They are here in America too, but some traveled to South Africa to mine diamonds. It was a long time ago and I don't believe they kept track of each other as thoroughly as your clan. They survived many hardships."

"The ones who left must have been terrified. The clan had never strayed. For millions of years they lived in their land, secluded from most of the world. Over time the world grew smaller and the clan larger. There were more sightings of jaguars in the vicinity. People were frightened and set out to hunt the cats. The families moved farther into the hills, but Scotland is not a large country and eventually there was nowhere to go." Lyn thought about her ancestors who had such great courage.

"I think terrified might be an exaggeration. Some men have the wandering gene in their bodies and they search for new places, excited by the prospect and ready to see new things and experience other cultures," Deacon's voice was soft yet gave assurance.

"I will never understand that. I like my home and I have no thoughts of exploring uncharted territories." She sipped her wine then set the glass on the table, staring at the red liquid and wondering about her future—their future if they were to have one. Would she have to leave Cactus Junction to be with him, and would he want to explore the world?

"But a little traveling?" his eyebrow rose a fraction. "Wouldn't that be fun? When this is over we can sightsee. I've wanted to watch the sun set from Oia in Santorini and at the Temple of Poseidon. The ocean is so blue and when the sun is going down, the water turns a silver color."

Lyn laughed. "Why you're a romantic at heart. Yes, traveling is fine as long as I have my little spot in Cactus Junction to come home to. I do not have the lust for wandering."

"Not an adventuress, that's good to know." He pulled her close for a tight hug then let her go.

With a quick sip of wine, Lyn continued the tale, "The reasons for leaving their homeland weren't just wanderlust, but finding mates. Alistair had not found his wife and he had constant dreams of the land across the ocean. A face with amber colored eyes and hair the color of a raven's wing haunted him. He left Scotland in hopes of finding this woman. Five men and two women set out together and founded a settlement in Texas."

"Texas is a big state with lots of room, but I'm guessing some must have branched out."

"They did. My family settled, as you know, in the Sierra Madres. My great grandfather is of the Apacheria, but everyone else is Scottish. I'm not sure how that happened."

"It was preordained." His voice was casual yet his shoulders and body were tense. "The story was written in the stars and is as old as time."

"Written in the stars?" she parroted. "I have questions. My brothers believe that story but..."

"You're not sure you do," he finished for her, cocking his head to one side in a gesture she was growing to love.

She turned, one hand on his chest, thinking about what he'd said and her feelings for this man as well as the dreams she'd had about him, with him. "I'm not really sure about anything anymore. I just want to let life happen and right now we have bigger issues to worry about."

"That's interesting and you're right about the larger picture. We have bigger fish to fry." He wrapped his arms around her, his hands on her back, pulling her close then bending toward her. His lips found hers and he traced the seam of her mouth with his tongue.

"Ummm...." she opened for him, letting his tongue slip inside to dance with hers. His kiss held so much passion and feelings so intense, she wanted to melt inside him and become one with him. She'd never been kissed like this before and knew he was the only one who could elicit this intense emotion. She returned the kiss, then wrapping her arms around his neck, pulled him closer.

Her fingers wove into his hair and she let her tongue slip inside his mouth, touching his teeth and tongue. Waves of heat ignited inside her and she wanted him more than she'd ever wanted anyone or anything.

He ran his hands down her back, then up, pulling her body closer as if any space between them was too much. She slipped her hands beneath his shirt and felt the raw power of the man. His muscles rippled as she touched him. She wanted to pull his shirt over his head and feel all of him next to her flesh. With her eyes closed, the vivid memory of his face while she lay in the sweat lodge flashed through her head then vanished with her escalating physical needs.

He groaned and deepened the kiss, their tongues dueling, tasting, touching, needing fulfillment. Time seemed to standstill as all her dreams appeared to be rushing to a pinnacle and all she had to do was say yes and accept this man into her life, accept the intimacy she craved and accept him as her soul mate.

She wasn't ready to commit just yet, but perhaps she could handle intimacy.

He finished the kiss, pulling back then looking at her and all-knowing-smile on his chiseled bronzed features. "We shouldn't go too fast or too soon. We have a lifetime to discover everything about each other. I plan on knowing you intimately and I hope you want the same."

"But..." Now she wasn't ready to stop. She wanted this kiss, then another and wherever that kiss might lead. Yet she knew he was right even though she didn't want to admit anything.

"Hush," he told her. "I want to make love to you but we have unfinished business and I don't want sex between us to cloud our judgment." He traced her jawline with a fingertip, a smile on his handsome face, his eyes twinkling with humor or love...

Lyn turned away in a feeble attempt to hide her emotions from him, but she sensed he could read her thoughts before she spoke them. Her body throbbed, her insides on fire with need, and he stopped. She couldn't believe he'd brought her to this intensity in such a short time. Everything about him was raw and passionate--primal.

"I believe," she inhaled a deep steadying breath, "You have too much control and I'm not sure I like it."

"Where you are concerned, Sugar, I have no control. If we had continued for one more millisecond, I would not have been able to stop myself. I want you more than I want my next breath of air."

Wishing she'd gone with her gut instinct and pulled him closer when she'd had the chance; Lyn leaned back, crossing her arms in front of her, a downward turn to her mouth. "What do we do now? Sit and talk? Sip more wine? I'm not sure where to go with all of this."

"Find out as much as we can about the poachers, and lie low until we get word from Brody about the demon that is after you."

"Lie low..." her head spun with thoughts of them between the bed sheets. Pursing her lips and furrowing her brows in what she knew was considered a frown, she rose and walked to the window, glass of wine in hand. Her thoughts so jumbled she didn't know what to think or believe. She wanted to solve the problem, attack, but the offense she knew was a good defense.

Don't race off and get yourself into trouble just because you're impatient, girlfriend. Patience.

"Lie low," he parroted.

"I don't like waiting. I want to do something. This is all so frustrating." She walked to the kitchen and rummaged through the cupboards, then turned away. "I get nervous when I can't be proactive. And when I get nervous and frustrated, I eat. I don't want to eat. If this keeps up, when I leave here I'll have gained ten pounds. Sheesh."

"What do you have in mind and it better not be dangerous. I won't let you risk yourself." His voice held the same note of command she'd heard earlier when they were in Vegas.

"I don't think you brought a laptop, so we're going to have to find an internet café where we can google information about the poachers." She rose to walk to the bedroom, pausing at the doorway then turning around to watch him.

"Googling I can handle. Tomorrow then," he told her, hanging back even though she sensed he wanted to follow her and wrap his arms around her. "But I do know a few things. I doubt if they put their address out there in cyberspace, but there has to be a way to locate them."

She thought about what he said. "We could go back to the forest and have a look around."

"Maybe, but that might put you in harm's way," he paused, a scowl marring his features, but didn't say anything else.

She wanted to make love with him, not talk about poachers, and she wondered if she could seduce him, but then she'd be tricking him, and she didn't want their relationship to start out that way.

"You know, poachers won't find us as long as we stay in human form. We really don't have anything to be afraid of." Her argument was sound. Venturing into the forest might well be the fastest way to locate the poachers.

"True, the tiger is an endangered species." He rose and strode toward her, pulling her into his arms once more. "And shapeshifters even more endangered."

He pulled her against him, running his hands down her back. "Why would anyone want to hunt and kill them? They are so beautiful. You are so beautiful."

She turned in his arms, sure this time if he tried to kiss her, she wouldn't let him move away from her.

"One reason—a million reasons," he began to list them. "Valuable pelts, parts used in medicine and folk remedies and tiger bone wine..."

"That's horrible." Lyn's body shuddered against his strength. "And you think it was poachers today who were after us?" They had come so close to dying. She wanted to feel renewed and alive. "I would like to see them all die a horrible death."

"You want to torture these men?"

She nodded and felt his hands stroking her arms. "My little tiger, I would never want to tame you."

"I'm already tame." She laughed, knowing she wasn't, but she had been subdued by the Amazonian Devil. With that fight, she'd realized life did not go on forever, and she should never take anything for granted. Rushing into danger was a thing of her past not her future. She understood she was not invincible. Plans must be made, caution and safety needed to be considered. She was not foolish or stupid.

He took her hand and led her onto the balcony and away from the temptation of the bedroom. A slight breeze blew off the bay and a bright moon hung low in the sky. The velvet of the night was sprinkled with stars. She let the breeze sift through her and caress her skin.

"You know you're not tamed, but I'm glad you don't want to take a lot of risks with your life. I would worry endlessly if you did."

"I'm hungry." She needed to change the subject. "Let's go for a walk and see if we can find somewhere that is still open to get something to eat."

"It's past midnight."

"Don't tell me you can't be tempted by some good food." She poked at his stomach. She wasn't sure if the diversion would work, but it was worth a try.

"I'm happy foraging through the cupboards for something." He looked from her to the inside.

"We both know there is nothing in them. We ate all of the popcorn, and the bottle of wine is empty."

"You're going to have to get dressed, you know. And I'm against that." He viewed her up and down with a look of appreciation.

"Okay, then we can stay here and eat popcorn. I was just bored and I am a little hungry and I don't want to sleep, and..." *I want him to kiss me and hold me close, and I want him to make love to me. If we stay here I'm going to go out of my mind.*

"Come on," he gave in, "Let's see what we can find."

~ * ~

Deacon had never felt as ill at ease as he did at this moment. When she'd showered, he'd heard from Brody. Some of the clan watched the roads and they'd expected Balor anytime, but he hadn't shown up yet because he was lost in the desert. The plan was to terrorize him then kill him. They would have to find him first.

They couldn't fight and defeat a ghost and so far that's what Balor was; transparent. He'd been spotted on a back road near Vegas, but after that he'd not been seen or heard from. His family had scouts located at various spots along the road to Cactus Junction. There was only one way to get in and out, except by air. To the best of his knowledge, Balor didn't have that ability and neither did the sea demons.

Looking at the door where Lyn had disappeared to change clothes, he waited impatiently. A few minutes ago, he'd come so close to scooping her into his arms and marching into the bedroom with her. It had taken all of his control to stop from giving into his sexual desires.

He wanted her, yesterday, but he had to wait; had to make sure she wanted him as much as he did her. And he wasn't a man to rush her into bed even though he almost had. It was a good idea to go out again, for food, to be in the public eye where he couldn't make a fool of himself.

"I'm ready." She stood in the living room purse in hand and dressed in the skinny jeans and a loose top that slid off her shoulder, leaving him staring open-mouthed at the revealed skin. Those clothes were among the few he'd purchased before hand.

"Where do you want to go?" He offered his arm as they left the room and he locked the door behind them. Instead of taking the elevator, they walked down the staircase to the main floor.

"Anywhere. I want a nice glass of wine and something else..."

"Something else?" He knew the something else he wanted. He wanted her naked and in bed with him, but that wasn't going to happen so he'd have to satisfy himself with holding hands and looking into her eyes.

She shrugged her slim shoulders and the shirt dropped off her other shoulder. His body shuddered with need, flesh jumping to life. Thoughts of kissing her raced through his head, but if he tried that approach, they wouldn't leave the room until morning light.

"I guess I'm not as hungry as I thought. Maybe some fries and Tzatziki sauce to go with them."

"Okay," he was willing to give her anything she wanted. They walked outside arm in arm. People roamed from place to place. A group of young men were singing and vendors who had earlier tried to coax people into their stores were all closed for the night.

They found seats in a little café about a quarter mile from their hotel and sat down. A boy of about twelve came by trying to sell them a hand held sewing machine, the clicking resounding in her ear, then a young woman wanted Deacon to purchase a flower for her.

Lyn shook her head and Deacon told them no, but they kept trying until both turned their backs and ignored them, giving the vendors incentive to move on to others who might be more vulnerable.

The wine and fries were served. Deacon sat back, watching Lyn and loving everything about her. She was one of a kind: spunky, sweet, sexy, funny, and beautiful. He wondered what she thought of him. Just looking at her gave him carnal thoughts best left for the bedroom, which they hadn't ventured into together. They would soon though. He knew he couldn't keep his hands to himself for much longer.

"I wonder if we can find these people we're looking for on our own without sending out fliers that we're looking for them."

"The poachers?" she asked, dipping a fry into the cucumber and yogurt sauce, her favorite.

"Yeah."

"We can spend some time hiking. I'm pretty sure they'll be back too." He drummed his fingers on the table while he thought. "We need to be careful. There are probably traps set that anyone could wander into."

She put her hand down, a fry hovering inches from the table. "They wouldn't set them on the hiking trails?"

"No, but just off the paths and maybe around the narrower animal trails." His hatred simmered.

"That's barbaric."

"I know." He gazed out at the fort sitting in the bay. Water lapped around the shoreline, and if they didn't have so much to worry about, this would be idyllic and so romantic. The fort that had been built to guard the bay had once been a hotel. Now there were boats that could take tourists out to see it. Perhaps they should do that. It might be a nice diversion.

"I'm changing the subject." She gave warning. "What about Balor? Is it safe?" She pulled her shirt, which had slipped again, back to cover her shoulder.

"While you were showering, I spoke to Brody. They have spotted the demon. He is trying to find Cactus Junction, but it seems he's lost and wandering around the hills, so until Brody tells us he's found him, we need to expect him to show up here."

"He couldn't possibly know we are here. There is no paper trail, no airline tickets, nothing."

"I know but we can't be cocky. Arrogance could mean your life."

"Okay," she dipped another fry in the sauce, "We can get up early, buy a prepared lunch, and head back into the woods."

"How early is early? And what about the Internet café?" He wanted to sleep in but only if she lay beside him and that wasn't going to happen tonight. He couldn't risk losing focus.

"Before noon." She laughed, eating the fry, then swirling her wine around in the glass before taking a drink.

"Works for me. And before it gets too hot."

"That too. What will we be looking for?"

Deacon paused, fry mid air, "Poisoned water, traps of any kind and anything appearing suspicious."

"This time seems to idyllic, almost unreal." Lyn stared at Deacon. "I don't like what my gut is telling me—the thoughts flying through my head terrify. Demons, poachers, when will it all end?"

"Nothing is going to happen." He wanted to reassure her. Taking her hand in his, he rubbed the knuckles then brought it up to place a tender kiss on the top then another. *Stop now while you can think straight.*

"You don't need to lie to me. I understand the trouble, and I felt the fear today, knew the threat."

"I'm not. I will never lie to you. If I thought there would be any danger for us tomorrow, we wouldn't go."

"If you saw a person who was a shifter, would you know?"

Her questioned startled him. He kissed her hand again, not wanting to let it go. "I would if the shifter was a tiger. How about you?"

"Would you? Can you be so sure? I'm not positive I would know." She was shaking her head and rambling. "I don't think so. I don't know. I guess I never have had the opportunity. I didn't know you were."

"I believe it's a given. You just haven't honed your skills. You've lived a sheltered life in Cactus Junction, and I think that's what your parents intended."

"Have you sensed anyone here?" She pulled her hand back and set it in her lap, protecting herself from herself and searching the surrounding people as if she could tell just by looking at them.

"I've sensed a few but haven't been able to pinpoint them," he told her as he too glanced around.

"It kind of makes me feel like a sitting duck with the shifters circling around us." She looked over shoulder as if one stood behind her and was waiting to pounce. "I don't like the feeling."

"They are going to be friendly, cautious at first, wouldn't you be?" He leaned back in the chair and gazed through the few people. The crowds were growing smaller and he knew as the hour grew later, they should leave too. But again, and for what reason he could only speculate. His gut told him to stay.

"What I do know is that I would never approach someone I didn't know. I would have never gone with you, except you didn't exactly give me a choice." Her voice faded while she gazed at the rough stone beneath the table.

"No, I didn't. The time was a factor. There was none. Explanations had to come later," he told her deadpan. "We didn't have one minute to spare. Balor was on our heels."

"Excuse me." A tall dark haired man, lean yet muscular in build, stood beside the table, speaking softly. His green eyes seemed to pierce through her. "I think we need to talk."

"Do we?" Deacon meant for caution to be the main factor in this discussion. He knew this man was the shifter who had been circling their table for the last fifteen minutes. Diligently, he'd watched him just as the man had studied him. They were dancing the two of them, each waiting for the other to show his cards.

"May I sit?"

"I'm not sure," Deacon answered. "Why are you here?"

"I believe you know why." His voice was low and steady, almost a growl. "Your presence has shifted the balance of power here and you must make amends."

Lyn rubbed her arms as if a chill had swept through her.

"Tell me." Deacon motioned for the man to sit before nodding to a waiter. "Do you want anything?"

The man looked up and nodded. "A beer."

The waiter left and returned a few minutes later. They were all silent until they had the privacy Deacon wanted.

"You're a shifter, but you're not from around here." The man sounded accusatory, which surprised Deacon.

"No, I'm not. What is it you want?"

"The same thing you do," the man said.

"First, I'd like to learn your name. I'm Deacon McClain." Deacon held his hand out.

"Jonathan Stewart." He looked at Lyn.

She cleared her throat and holding out her hand said, "Lyn McKenna."

"Now, what is it you want from us and why did you wait so long to introduce yourself?" Deacon didn't want to be wary of this man, but he was.

"You were in the woods this morning and were almost killed by poachers. We have rules around here, and the two of you broke most of them within ten minutes."

"Really..." Deacon didn't have any idea where this conversation was going. Rules? How the hell was he supposed to know anything about rules?

"We were so close," Jonathan shook his head. "So close—until the two of you changed everything."

"Close too what?" Lyn asked.

"The poachers would have left in a few days except for the two of you giving them reason to stay. We who live her are so cautious. We have to be in order to survive. You've upset the balance."

Deacon nodded. "Yes, I see, but we had no idea there were actually poachers in the area. No one put up warning signs."

"Why are you in Nafplio?" Jonathan's voice once again turned into an angry growl.

"That's not your concern," Deacon told him, eyeing him suspiciously, yet knowing his question was important.

"It is when you put my clan in danger." Jonathan's jaw stiffened.

"I understand and we won't do it again. I promise."

"Stay out of the woods and off the hiking paths." Jonathan spoke in low warning tones.

"I can't do that."

"Of course you can."

"We just want to help." Lyn spoke up. "We'd like to stop these criminal gangs here before they leave and find others to kill whether they are shifters or normal tigers."

"What do you care?"

"She may not be a tiger, but she is also a shifter." It was Deacon's turn to put menace in his voice.

"She is?" Jonathan looked surprised.

"Jaguar," Lyn said.

Jonathan nodded, his gaze raking over her as if inspecting her.

"And my mate." Deacon gave his own warning growl.

"Really?" Lyn stood hands on hips. "We haven't determined that yet and it's private."

"He had to tell us. We cannot risk infiltration of our ranks."

Jonathan held out his hands. "Settle down, I mean no disrespect. I get it that the two of you want to help, but the clan voted and decided to stay in seclusion until they moved on."

"To another place to kill more tigers?" Lyn's tone sarcastic. "I don't think so. Wouldn't it be best to end them here and now?"

"We can't stop them. There are two many and the money will just bring more evil men hunting tigers."

"I understand, but we have no choice. As you say, more will come, but we have to unite and fight them. We cannot hide."

"Well," Jonathan snorted. "That's easy for you to say. You're not a tiger."

"You're right, but I do understand evil and all evil must be confronted. If we don't fight, they win," Lyn said.

"We could argue for days," Jonathan countered.

"And you cannot tell me what to do or what not to do. We are going to fight these men." Lyn stiffened.

"Very well, come to a meeting of my clan. Talk to all and get them to join in your fight."

"When?" Deacon didn't like the tone of this conversation, but he felt there was no choice. They would have to go and meet his clan.

"Tomorrow at four. I will set it up with the elders of the clan. I will explain what you do and the fight you say must happen here in our domain."

"We will be there." Deacon rose, holding out his hand.

"Bring your lady and don't go into the forest tomorrow," Jonathan warned.

"We have to go and explore. If we do, we will have more information for your clan. We need to understand who we are dealing with." Deacon wasn't going to let someone dictate to him, but he did mean to discover more about this man and his people.

"I understand, even though I don't like what you are telling me," Jonathan acknowledged with one more glance at Lyn.

"We will be careful and we won't shift. I don't want to put my life on the line or jeopardize a single person of your clan. We need to keep everyone safe. Unless one of the poachers is a tiger shifter, they will never think we are anything but tourists hiking around the bay.

"You'd better keep your promise."

~ * ~

Brody paced while Carr and Kimi watched.

"What's got you so riled?" Carr stood, wiping his sweaty hands on his jeans. "Thought you'd be the calm one here."

"I haven't heard from Deacon since yesterday and with only one sighting of Balor, I'm not sure where all of this is headed," Brody worried. Anything could have happened to his sister and he didn't like not knowing, not being there to protect her. What the hell was going on and why hadn't Deacon called him?

"What? Now you don't trust the man? You were the one who sent them to the far reaches of the planet. I hope you, at least, know where they are." Carr poured himself a glass of water from a pitcher sitting nearby.

"I do trust Deacon. I'm just worried and I half expected a call this morning, but I also understand calls can be traced. I'm just not sure if, from what I've heard about Balor, he has the know how to do something like that."

"Yeah," Carr began with a laugh. "He's an ancient demon who has recently been resurrected. Doubt if he knows anything about computer hacking, or tracing cell phones."

"I live in this world and I couldn't hack into a computer," Kimi voiced her opinion as she walked into the room. "I don't understand what all of you are so worried about. I think it's more important we stay in contact and know where she is. I've never been separated from her for this long."

"And you could be right." Brody ran his hands through his hair. "I'd feel better if we put Balor back where he belongs."

"Dead," Lyn said.

"Dead," Carr mimicked.

Guy stepped into the room, hat in hand and a frown marring his face.

"What's up?" Carr turned his attention to his younger sibling.

"Balor has been spotted in an old beat up junk-heap of a car. It's stalled about a half mile out of town. Want me to pick him up?"

"Not by yourself," Brody spoke up.

"All right then, whose game to come along and what do we do when we find him? Kill him?"

That sounded so cutthroat, but they all knew in order to keep Lyn safe that's what would happen. Still they couldn't just shoot him, could they? They had to give him a chance to renounce the sea demons that sent him to find Lyn and bring her back to sacrifice.

Carr looked at Brody who was staring at him, then Brody spoke, "Goes against everything we believe in to kill."

"Bring him in for questioning. Maybe there's another way." Carr needed to take charge. It was his sole responsibility to guard the clan's reputation, worldwide, and he understood his word was the law even if Brody disagreed with him and he sure as hell hoped Brody would see things his way.

Guy nodded.

"We'll both come with you." Brody volunteered, not wanting to risk any of his siblings.

"Yup, saddle up the tow truck and let's see what kind of creature this Balor really is." Carr glanced at Brody as if waiting for him to change his mind.

"Don't take any chances." Kimi stood and watched her three brothers leave the room. A second later she ran after them and gave each a hug. "I'd like to go with you," she whispered.

"Not on your life," Guy answered for all of them.

Margo, Carr's mate and Sadie, Brody's mate, stepped into the hallway to give reassuring hugs.

"It's going to turn out just fine," Sadie said. "We'll wait with you, hold hands and pretend we're not petrified."

"Go on," Margo waved them toward the front door. "Do what you have to. Bottom line, this demon, Balor, has to be defeated. We'll be here when you return with the demon or not with him."

Carr pulled Margo close and kissed her, loving the feel of his woman in his arms. He'd move heaven and earth and whatever else he needed to move to keep his sister alive. He'd never forget how close he and Margo had come to death at the hands of the ice demon, Jokul. His sister wasn't going to live through a terror so intense and so close that she'd jump at every shadow. He would end Balor if necessary, yet he prayed for another way. He gave her one last kiss on the cheek before turning away and heading outside.

Brody wrapped an arm around Sadie and walked with her to the door then he, too, kissed his wife. "I love you."

"I love you too, be careful." Sadie pushed him away as she wiped a lone tear from beneath her eye. "I hate watching you walk into danger." With that said, she turned and strode into the house.

Carr emerged and the three men hopped into the tow truck and revved up the engine.

"Where is he?" Carr asked, leaning back and trying to visualize what the trio would do. What would they do? End him? Put him in a place where he couldn't escape? Neither of those solutions set well with him.

"Half mile down the road by the rock formation that sticks up like a sore thumb." Guy stepped on the gas.

"How do you want to approach him?" Carr still looked to Brody for answers even though he possessed more power that his older sibling.

"Carefully," Brody laughed. "Really, we just need to be cautious and try to talk to him. See what he thinks and if we can trust him. Don't know what kind of guy we're dealing with. If he fails the questions or the tests, I gather it means he'll lose his life."

"If the sea demons catch up to him," Guy said.

"Maybe we can offer him sanctuary," Brody added.

"And if you do that, Lyn will never believe she can come home." Carr didn't like the direction this conversation was going. Their sister needed to feel safe in Cactus Junction.

"What other options do we have?" Guy asked.

"He needs to die," Brody said; his emotions clear.

Chapter Five

Lyn wandered from her bed to the living room of the tiny condo they rented. A smile crossed her face when she saw Deacon sprawled on the couch, his left foot hanging over the end and his right foot resting on the floor. He groaned, rolling over and pulling covers from the floor to cover his partially nude body. She wondered why he hadn't used the second bedroom.

Trying not to wake him, she placed each foot carefully in front of her. Level with his chest, he reached out and stopped her, holding on to her leg.

"Oh! My god." Her heart leapt to her throat. "You scared me have to death." She knew first hand how that felt.

"I'm sorry. Reflexes. I'm not always a Neanderthal." Deacon sat up rubbing his eyes then face. "I need to shave."

No, he didn't. She liked him this way. He looked sexy and tempting with his shadow. "Thought you were asleep and was trying to get by you without waking you up."

"Didn't mean to frighten you. I fell asleep on the couch." He maneuvered, keeping the blanket draped over him.

"Want some coffee?" Lyn thought it prudent to change the topic at least in her mind and before she had to look at his abs and rippling muscles any longer. If she busied herself in the kitchen, her back would be to him. A prudent idea and one she meant to implement.

"Sure," he rose keeping the blanket in discreet places. "I'll go shower then dress. Be back in a minute."

Tugging at her shirt to keep herself decent, Lyn opened the Nescafé and put the water on to boil. Humming to herself she waited then decided the water wouldn't bubble if she watched it. Outside a summer sun had just risen above the hills surrounding the bay and the sky was mottled with varying shades of pink and coral. A few high clouds stretched in thin waves and birds sang a constant medley of varying sounds.

The whistle on the kettle sounded the alarm that the water was ready. She walked inside and put coffee crystals in the cups then the water, stirring each one.

"Coffee's ready." She stood near the bathroom door with her cup in hand then returned to the fresh air of the Greek seacoast.

Birds flew overhead and peacefulness of the morning filled her with serenity. She felt as if anything could be accomplished. Her entire life ahead of her, she realized she wanted to spend it with Deacon. *What an epiphany.* He must be her soul mate.

"Mornin', Sugar. You really shouldn't tempt me so..." He touched her bare leg with the top his hand then let it settle there, his thumb rubbing gentle circles and his eyes telling her how much he wanted her.

It warmed her heart. "What if I want to tempt you—Sugar," she challenged him, needing to know if he felt the same things she did. She knew he thought of her as his mate. He'd intimated the fact several times but he'd never acted on it or come right out and told her. A distinct possibility existed that he didn't feel any sexual attraction for her.

He ignored her, looking toward the pool and the lone swimmer doing laps. Silence stretched forever. She cleared her throat, needing to curl up inside herself and hide.

Deacon leaned forward, a fingertip beneath her chin, his eyes focused on hers. "Listen to me, Sugar. I want you. Don't you ever forget that but we have so much to figure out before I make love to you. I don't want our feelings complicated with the danger we face. When this is all over, we will explore every possibility and see what lies between us."

"So, you're not so sure about this mate thing either..."

"I'm not, but what I am sure of is that there is something very tangible between us. We connect in ways I would have never imagined."

She sucked in her lip then gazed at him. "All right then. Okay, I'm not sure of things either." She sipped her coffee, feeling tears well in the back of her throat. After that little declaration, she didn't feel as big a fool, but there was still so much indecision. She wasn't one to share the secrets of her heart and here she'd blurted out, or practically blurted them out, to a man she'd known little more than two days.

"You don't sound as if I explained myself very well."

"Where do we start?" Shifting her thoughts to something else might make her forget her feelings.

"Breakfast," he said. "It's always good to start the day off with a meal. A person thinks betters with a full stomach."

"Shower first and I should probably put a few more clothes on. Should I prepare for a hike?"

He nodded, looking pensive, his mind seeming to be a million miles away. She wanted to ask him what he was thinking about but decided against it. His thoughts might not be something she needed or wanted to hear.

Entering her room, she turned to look over her shoulder at him. With a sigh she closed the door. The shower was hot and soothing against her tired, sore muscles. She turned the water hotter, letting it beat against her shoulders. Closing her eyes, she absorbed the warmth for a few more minutes. Soaking in a hot tub sounded like a wonderful idea, but that wasn't going to be possible.

She emerged ready for a day hike to see Deacon on the phone. He looked up and smiled at her, motioning for her to sit. He spoke to the unknown person on the other end, the conversation seeming endless.

Before meeting him on the couch, she made two more coffees. She set one on the table for Deacon and held on to the other, sipping as she watched and listened to the one-sided conversation.

When Lyn had first seen him on the phone, she'd hoped it was Brody telling him they'd taken care of Balor and it was safe to return to Cactus

Junction. But it didn't take long to figure out her big brother was not on the other end of the line. One thing for sure, he knew the person well.

The conversation continued for a few more minutes until she heard Deacon say his goodbyes and turn his cell phone off.

"Who..."

"My family in Ireland."

"Oh." That came as a surprise and she didn't know why. If Deacon McClain was her mate, then of course his family would be involved.

"My dad, Sean. He's concerned about all of this and has been in contact with your brother, Brody. He has headed to Cactus Junction."

"Oh." Lyn was at a loss and didn't know what to think. "Why? Why would he go to my hometown?"

"Isn't it obvious? Because we look after our own, just as your family does."

She breathed in deeply. "I just don't want to think the McKennas need reinforcement."

"Look, don't think of it that way."

Her thoughts and emotions were in turmoil. She rose and strode to the balcony, needing to sort this news out and understand. Without turning around she spoke, "And my brothers are okay with your father arriving?"

Deacon shrugged, "I don't know. Dad didn't tell me what your brother's said, but I believe he can be of some help."

She swiveled around then leaned against the railing. "All right. Let's get something to eat."

"That's it?" he asked. "A few questions and you're ok with the news. I don't believe you."

"Yup." She walked to the front door and stood beside it waiting for him. "What choice do I have? I have to understand this situation calls for the unexpected."

He grinned, following with a lazy saunter that, for a few seconds, took her mind off the previous conversation.

They bought bread and fruit to eat as they walked. The day was going to be warm but in the shelter of the forest they would find shade and a cooling breeze. She didn't know what they'd discover or what to expect, but anything was better than waiting.

Silence built a barrier between them. The questions Lyn wanted to ask felt strange. Why should she be suspect of his family helping hers? Uneasiness settled in the pit of her stomach. At the moment she felt as if the mission they were on was impossible.

Why and or how would they find the poachers?

If there were poachers.

The trail appeared much the same as it had the previous day. She saw and heard nothing that seemed strange or out of place.

"What are you thinking?" Deacon stopped following Lyn and stepped beside her, his hand resting on her shoulder.

"Convoluted thoughts. I don't know. It seems all the elements in the world are after me—us. A few days ago my life was normal and now it's all crazy like. I want to be able to think about you—about us without finding myself in a life and death situation."

"Your life will be normal again. I promise you." His smile settled in her heart even though she knew he was just trying to reassure.

"I suppose." She shrugged off his attempt to console. "I don't like playing the waiting game, and that's what we are doing."

"I don't like it either. Look..." he pointed to a place off the trail.

"What? I don't see anything."

"Look closer, Sugar." His voice had taken on an urgent tone, and while he waited for her to observe and tell him what had peaked his interest, his gaze seemed to roam the terrain.

She squatted for a closer look. "I see a twig."

"Exactly."

"I don't get it."

"If you were in your cat form would you step on it?" His query sounded urgent and he now spoke in a whisper.

She looked at him quizzically then, "No, but what does it matter?"

"Neither would any large cat and the poacher's understand this fact." Deacon moved close and with a stick he pushed the debris away from the spot directly behind the stick.

In a hole she saw an iron trap connected to chain. Her heart lodged in her throat and she couldn't speak. Blood seemed to drain from her body at the realization of what she saw.

"Lyn, prepare yourself. We are about to meet someone." His voice was whisper soft but held a menace she'd never heard before. She could just imagine what he was thinking, knowing it had to be close to her thoughts.

"What are you doing? That's private property." The voice came from behind them.

Lyn froze and Deacon swiveled as if in slow motion. "We didn't mean to intrude." Deacon spoke easily as if he didn't care what was happening here. That he'd discovered a poacher's trap meant to put a tiger in such stress there would be no recovery, and that the tigers this man tried to snare were also human.

This man was despicable, horrible. No list of adjectives could describe him, yet Lyn tried.

"You need to leave," the man told them.

"This isn't private property," Deacon persisted and after a long silence, he said, "We might have a common goal."

"We have nothing in common."

"But maybe we do," Deacon's voice held a distinctive growl, frightening and had Lyn stepping back suddenly afraid of him. This was a side of Deacon he'd never shown her.

The man seemed cautious but curious, moving forward, his eyes gleaming with an emotion Lyn couldn't decipher, but knew she didn't like.

"I doubt it."

With a boldness Lyn wasn't sure she approved of, Deacon said, "I know what you are doing here." And she suddenly wanted to stand up to this man, put him in jail where he belonged. Her activist self seemed to resurface against her will, but she didn't want to suppress it any longer.

"You've set traps. It's damn illegal and the jail time and fines are huge. Do you really want to set me loose to expose you? I could do that—put you away. Then where would you be? In jail." Deacon stood tall, his height overpowering the man who stood in front of him. Intimidating would not come close to describing how he looked. It seemed to Lyn he was part tiger part human only he was now in human form.

"I could have you killed." The man spoke in a monotone, deliberate and threatening.

Deacon's smile intimidated, his presence frightened, and his voice held an unspoken warning. "And I could kill you."

The man stepped back, his hand resting on the gun at his hip. "You don't know who you threaten."

"I know and I don't want to kill you. I want part of your profits."

~ * ~

Deacon had never regretted any conversation he'd had before more than he regretted this one, but he had to take advantage of the unforeseen confrontation. He felt dirty. He'd half expected to find Jonathan in the forest, stalking him, overseeing his every move, instead he'd found one of the poachers. Now he had to find a way inside this group.

He watched as the man stepped backward as if thoughts of running swept through his head. A moment later the man stiffened, his jaw line hardening and his lips thinning.

"Why should I trust you?" He pulled out the gun, his hand quivering as he pointed it in Deacon's direction.

Deacon stood, feet apart, arms crossed in front of him as if the gesture could ward off the bullet. "Because I want what you want." Was his simple answer.

"Proof? I need proof. Why would I believe you?"

Deacon spread his arms wide. "I have none, except my word. Trust me."

Lyn watched him wide-eyed. Deacon didn't like the wary look in her eyes and prayed she'd follow his lead. This wasn't a situation he wanted her in the middle of but here they were.

"Deacon..."

"Hush, this will work out. Let my wife go home and I'll talk to you." Deacon nodded his head toward Lyn.

The man's sinister grin sent a chill down his spine. "She's my leverage. She ain't goin' nowhere."

That thought didn't sit right, but he couldn't think of any way to change the man's words. Lyn would play it cool. She was a daredevil at heart, loving the game as well as the risks.

"I want in on the money too, but what are you trapping?" She moved closer to the snare.

"Don't get so close," Deacon warned, stretching his hand out to stop her forward progress, terrified she'd get caught in the lethal trap.

She moved back and looked up with innocent blue eyes. "Why?"

"Because you could spring it," the man with the gun motioned for her to move away.

"We all know what that snare is set for. There's been sightings of tigers around here and a jaguar, white ones, both of them. Their pelts will bring a lot of money."

"That looks painful." Lyn pointed at the snare, grimacing. "Can't you just shoot them?"

"And ruin the pelt?" the man answered as if she were stupid. "No way would anyone shoot what got caught in one of those traps.

"Oh," she said. "I didn't know."

"What's goin' on here?" Jonathan appeared ahead of them, sauntering down the trail as if he owned it.

Well, he'd expected to see Jonathan sooner than later. Now there was another wild card in the mix and Deacon really needed to get Lyn away. He held his breath for a few minutes, hoping it would help him think.

The man put his gun in his back waistband and covered it with his shirt. "Havin' a little chat with this man. Met him on the trail," Deacon said. "He's a hunter, big game, but we know there aren't any tigers in Greece."

Jonathan stopped, studying the man. "Really. Why aren't you in Africa or India?"

"Who are you to question this?" A few more men emerged from the bushes behind them.

"A friend and who are these people?" Jonathan asked, his hands balling into fists.

Deacon pulled out a card and handed it to the man. "Give me a call. Maybe we can meet and talk later. I think you will find I have assets you might want to use. Money...and I like to make more."

The man grunted, slipping the card into his pocket before turning and motioning his friends to walk down the trail.

The trio watched the poacher's retreating backs. Deacon's gut churned. The need to kill had never felt overpowering until this moment. What these men did was loathsome and inhumane.

Now he wanted to torture them as they did the big cats.

He took in a deep breath, crossing his arms over his chest. The poachers finally disappeared around a bend in the trail. A chill swept through Deacon and when he turned to face Jonathan, he was sure the man had the same sensation.

"Can we talk here?" Deacon knew there was a lot left unsaid and now that he'd met the poachers, there was a great deal to discuss.

"Better meet up at your place." Jonathan looked to the trap. "But first I have to tell the clan where this snare is. Don't want any one stepping on it, human or tiger form. And, I don't want to risk talking to you in public in case they have you followed."

"Can't you just rip it out?" Lyn rubbed her arms and looked at the place with disgust painted in her expression.

Jonathon waited a moment, silence clinging and seeming to vibrate the air. "Wish we could."

85

"The poachers would look to us first." Deacon spoke in low tones and watched her grumpy frown. "We're the only ones who know where this one is located."

"Let's go home. Maybe the man will call." Lyn started down the trail, her hips swinging provocatively with her quick-paced stride. The sight gave him a brief moment to smile and forget the perfidy going on here.

"Your woman's angry," Jonathan said with a little chuckle. "You'll have to find a way to make her feel better."

"Yeah, that she is." Deacon couldn't say how infuriated he was at what he saw and what now he was forced to leave. If the poachers hadn't seen him, he could have at least stuck a limb in the snare disabling it.

"Go, catch up to your woman." Jonathan motioned to him, following behind the pair.

Deacon jogged until he reached Lyn then slipped his arm around her, whispering in her ear. "We'll get them. I promise you." Then he kissed the lobe and blew on the damp spot, delighting in the tiny shiver he felt snaking through her body.

They reached the edge of town. Deacon pulled out another card and handed it to Jonathan. "Call me at eight. We can meet in my room." He gave him the address.

Lyn turned to Deacon, "I'm famished. I didn't realize we'd been away so long. And that conversation with the poacher..."

"We don't need to speak of it, but we do need to figure out how to catch them and bring them to justice." Deacon looked over his shoulder then down the street. Poachers could be anywhere. He didn't like this but he didn't have a choice.

"Can't we let the authorities do that?" Lyn sounded hopeful.

"We could and we will have to let them in on this as soon as we infiltrate the organization. I believe Jonathan's people have made some progress, and we don't want to get in their way or undermine anything they've been doing. You and I don't have any resources to track them and we do have the threat of Balor hanging over our heads."

"My head." She corrected him, leaning into his body and wrapping her arm around him.

"Well, I'm not going to argue, but if anything happens to you, I will die inside. So, I'm believin' it's my head too."

She snuggled in closer and he reveled in the feel of her body close to his. "Let's bring dinner home. We can relax, watch Greek television and eat."

She batted at him. "I don't understand Greek."

"We could watch the subtitles." He argued, wishing he could take this relationship to the next level.

"Really," she pulled back. "They have subtitles on the TV?"

"Doesn't everyone?" he queried.

"I don't know."

They walked in silence until they reached the café where they'd eaten the night before. Deacon ordered food, enough to last well into tomorrow if necessary. Apprehension seemed to swirl in evil circles around him. He was terrified for what was to come yet eager to confront the poachers. A good fight would ease the tension building between his shoulder blades.

A few minutes later, "Well, here we are, back in our room." Deacon set the food on the table in the dining room and pulled a chair out for Lyn before rummaging through the kitchen things for a corkscrew. Shit, but he was stupid. He should have thought to buy one when they were in the corner grocery store.

"What are you looking for?" Lyn emerged from the bedroom, dressed in sweat pants and a tank top, all her luscious curves beckoning him.

He didn't go for model skinny. Lyn fit all of his dreams physically and emotionally. In addition she was the brightest most intuitive woman he'd ever known.

"I am looking for the corkscrew and I don't think they have one. Should have stuck to the screw caps."

"You could break the neck on the counter. That might work." She laughed and opened another drawer, pulling the desired utensil from the back. "Saw it this morning when I was making coffee."

"That doesn't make sense." He reached for it and started opening the bottle.

"It does if you know what I was looking for?"

"Don't leave me hanging?" He poured wine in the glasses and handed one to her.

"A tea strainer. Thought I'd buy some tea leaves if they had one."

Opening the boxes, the food was still hot and steaming and smelled wonderful. Deacon bit into his Gyro and gave a grunt of satisfaction. Lyn pulled out a fry and ate it. He liked the easy silence between them, enjoyed being able to sit and watch her without conversation.

"Do they?" he asked.

"Do they what?" she paused, a bite of chicken half way to her mouth.

"A tea strainer."

"Oh, no they don't. What are we going to do about the poachers? Reading your body language..."

"My body language," he queried with a laugh. "What do you know about that?

"I know you're itching for a fight. That being cooped up in this room is making you miserable even though, except for sleeping we've barely been here."

"You've got me pegged," he told her. "I wanted to rip that poacher's throat out. You know the tigers that get caught in those traps die from stress and terror. I've heard stories of animals chewing their leg off to escape the trap, but they still can't escape the poachers."

"Maybe men like that is why we can shift. Maybe it's survival of the fittest. You know Darwin and all..."

"Hold that thought." Deacon answered his cell. "Jonathan?" He put it on speaker phone.

"We still good for eight?" Jonathan asked.

Chatter filled the background but Deacon couldn't make out what was said. "Yeah," he felt hesitant. "You comin' by yourself?"

"Like to bring my mate if that's okay."

Deacon felt the tension, knew this clan had been through more than anyone should. He felt a kinship with the tigers that could not shift, that couldn't protect themselves against the evil and greed that had made them an endangered species.

"Sure," he said.

"Can we bring anything?"

"Just yourselves and a plan, something that will end these poachers." Damn, he wished murder were legal. Bringing these men to justice would only slow the tide, it wouldn't end it.

"I'm trying." Jonathan's voice was muffled and that set Deacon's nerves on edge.

"What are you hiding?"

He heard the sigh on the other side of the line. "My children, they're terrified. We're thinking of moving somewhere if this doesn't put an end to the fear and the death."

"Okay, get here as soon as you can."

"His children," Lyn said. "That's horrible."

"It's an established clan. I don't know what to tell you, but could you spend most of your life in human form?"

"If I had to," Lyn said, refilling her glass.

"Of course you could. We all could but what would that accomplish?" He waved his hand around the room. "It's why we all find places where we can roam, where we can find solitude to be the people we really are. To feel safe from the outsiders who don't understand." He massaged his neck, trying to ease the ache that throbbed and would not go away. *From the people who want to make money at our destruction.*

Lyn set her glass on the table and walked to Deacon, rubbing his muscles, relieving the stress. "You don't have to protect the entire universe. You have my family, your family, these shifters who live here in Nafplio."

He turned and pulled her onto his lap, kissing her with a tenderness he'd never felt before. Every feeling with Lyn was new and different. He'd never dreamed he'd find his mate, and each time he saw her, touched her, talked to her, the emotions deepened.

"I need to protect you." He kissed her, his tongue meeting hers, melding and setting his body on fire. He didn't want to wait until all danger passed. He needed to renew the feeling of life. To feel whole, to feel one with his mate was a desperate need simmering inside his soul.

I wont' be complete until I love her fully.

Feeling her heartbeat in unison with his was imperative, compelling and a driving force in his survival.

She pulled away, touching his lips with a fingertip. "What is it?"

He shook his head, not wanting to tell her the depth of his feelings and how she'd become a part of him in such a short time. "It's nothing." He turned away from her piercing gaze.

"Liar."

Looking back at her he was at a complete and total loss. "I want to tell you I love you, but it's too soon. So I didn't just say that."

She touched his chin. "Deacon, I love you too." She bent down to kiss him, his hands sliding upward to her breast.

The knock on the door startled him and brought him back to reality. The reality that despite his feelings, they were still in grave danger from two directions.

She moved aside. There was nothing he could do about the significant bulge in his jeans. "I'm sorry." He kissed the tip of her nose before walking to the door.

"Who is it?"

"Jonathan and Cherise," came the voice from outside.

Deacon opened the door and the pair stepped inside.

~ * ~

A little while later Lyn and Deacon stepped inside Jonathan's home.

Jonathan and Cherise's living room was filled with men and women who supported the cause. They all wanted to protect their clan and the tiger population over the entire world.

90

"Welcome." Jonathan held out his hand in greeting, clasping Deacon's hand then shaking hands with Lyn. "Welcome to my home. Please find a seat."

Jonathan watched the couple sit, noting their apprehension. They'd seen the work of the poachers this afternoon, and he understood how devastating this knowledge could be.

"I hope we are going to do more than just talk." Deacon waved his hand at the group. "I'm new and I'm sure there are those of you who don't trust me just as I'm not willing to give my completely loyalty to this clan until I meet all of you."

Chatter sprang up around the room. Jonathan rose and held his hand up to silence the group. "Why don't you tell us something about you and your wife?"

Deacon smiled and Lyn frowned.

Deacon walked to the front of the room to stand by Jonathan. "I'm Deacon McClain, my clan lives in Ireland, but I'm sure that we are all related in some way. My father is Sean McClain."

Another round of chatter followed Deacon's announcement. While Sean was not a leader of the McClain clan, he was well known. He'd spent time traveling abroad and meeting others.

Deacon cleared his throat, pausing a minute to let the chatter come to a halt. "We did not come to Nafplio to become part of your group and bring the poachers to justice. We have other reasons for being here, but we inadvertently became involved when the poachers tried to kill us. So here we are."

"What about your woman?" Jonathan asked.

"She is my mate, but we haven't resolved that issue between us. This is Lyn McKenna. Her brother, Brody, is the head of the McKenna clan and her other brother, Carr, is the worldwide leader of all the McKennas."

"So the pair of you have impeccable credentials. Tell us why we should trust you."

"Trust must be earned," Lyn said. "But I will tell you this. We-" and she looked at Deacon then back to Jonathan, "-have only the desire to help. We run from our own demons, but we will take the time to bring the poachers to justice."

Once again the room broke out in chatter.

"What demons are those?" Cherise spoke up.

"We cannot say at the moment. Too much is at stake." Deacon looked to Lyn. "Her life is in jeopardy and we cannot risk a breach of confidence."

"So," Jonathan rocked back on his heels, "you expect us to share when you remain silent?"

"We do," Lyn offered. "For the time."

"We can't trust them," one of the clan members spoke up.

Jonathan waved his arm in the air. "We have no choice. Whether you like it or not, they are involved. Deacon's life is at stake from the poachers just as ours are. And Lyn, too."

"What about their secret?" Cherise asked. "I don't know why I should trust them. I need a reason, and if they're keeping things from us... Well, I don't like it."

"We will have to respect their silence as well as their secrets," a clan member said.

For a few more minutes the conversation as well as arguments took place around the room before the shifters came to an all encompassing silence.

"I believe we have come to a decision. Shall we vote?" Jonathan asked, searching the room for signs of discontent and finding none.

"All in favor of including Lyn and Deacon in our fight say aye."

The room resounded with the one word.

"Those apposed say nay."

One man spoke the single word and rose. "I have my doubts about these two, and I'm not ready to put my life in their hands, but if the rest of the clan believes their words, then I will go with the majority." He sat down.

"I guess the two of you are part of this group." Jonathan nodded toward Deacon and Lyn. "Now," he motioned to the group as a whole, "what are we going to do?"

The conversation grew lively again, everyone seeming to have an idea. Jonathan let them give and take ideas for several minutes before stepping in. "Lyn, Deacon and myself ran into a group of poachers this afternoon. They'd just set a trap on one of the trails out of the city. Deacon found it and was about to spring it when I came along."

The clan grew loud again.

"Why didn't you let him?" The question rang ominous in the tiny room, which seemed to grow smaller with each revelation.

"Because a man appeared, a man who was also a poacher. We couldn't risk letting him know that we didn't like what he did, and before we knew what was happening five more people emerged from the undergrowth."

"Oh..." was the collective reaction.

"We have to stop them." One man stood, walking to the window and turning, his agitation clear. "We have given up a part of our souls. We cannot shift and run with the wind. We have to hide in our homes and hope they will go away if there are no more sightings. They should be found and prosecuted."

"Has the World Wildlife Federation been notified?" another in the room asked.

"They have. And we wait for the expert guidance. I've been told they will send people. But you all must understand; tigers are not normally found in Greece. This is why we came here in the first place, and now it is working against us. I fear it will be far too dangerous for us to become vigilantes."

"You want us to wait for the WWF?" An angry clan member spoke from the back of the room.

"No, just as all of you have had enough. So have I. We try to catch them in their horrific deeds. There could be as few as three thousand two hundred tigers in the world. We can't sit by and watch our kind die."

"Then what?" someone asked.

"Deacon and Lyn have attempted to infiltrate the group. We wait and see what comes of this."

Chapter Six

"I feel as if I finally have a purpose," Lyn said as they walked through the outdoor cafés. She had a cause worth fighting for and a man she loved and was meant to be with through eternity.

"And what is that?" Deacon held fast to Lyn's hand. She felt the warmth as well as the security. His smile gave her reason to return it with a saucy grin.

She stopped walking and turned to him, one hand on his shoulder, her heart racing with the excitement sparked by today's events. "We can't talk about it now and you know it. We have to have privacy."

He groaned. "That's what I was afraid of and I don't like what I'm thinking. Sometimes it's better to say what's on your mind." He brought her hand to his lips and brushed a light kiss across them. "You chase danger..."

"Not like I did." She grinned, a spark of life surfacing for the first time since her encounter with the Amazonian Devil, and for the first time since that life changing experience, she felt alive. "And I promise I won't take any chances."

"You're damn right you won't." They turned the corner to move away from the cafés and crowds of people. He gave her hand a reassuring squeeze then let go to wrap his arm around her waist.

They stood in front of the condo, the night stretching on in front of them. Lyn turned and wrapped her hands around his neck, pulling him to her upturned face to initiate a kiss. She wanted to do this all day and this moment was her first opportunity.

Their lips met and touched, melded together. Inner warmth spiraled throughout her body. She licked her lips and kissed him again. His hands wrapped around her, pulling her closer until she felt his cock, hard against her. She smiled while she kissed him, realizing she could do that to him.

He kissed her again and again. She ran her fingers through his hair then down his neck and spine. "I want you; I need you more than life. You are my life," she breathed into his open mouth. Their tongues met and touched then danced together. God, how she needed him. Her emotions went way beyond the physical. She felt as if she were about to become one with him on a level only a shifter could understand.

"Let's take this inside." Then as if she weighed nothing at all, he scooped her into his arms and carried her, turning sideways to push the front door open before ascending the steps to their room.

He tried to kiss her as they walked upstairs, their lips touching for a fraction of a second. When he lifted his head, "Don't stop—please." She wiggled in his arms, her hands behind his head, pulling him closer.

"Have to get in the door." His words spoken in short little pants as he continued to place tender kisses on her face while ignoring her lips. "It's just going to take a second."

"Put me down then..." She couldn't believe she asked him to let go of her, but she had a different objective in mind.

"Not on your life. I'm not letting go of you--ever." The door swung open and they stepped inside, Deacon heading straight to the bedroom after shutting the door with his foot and letting Lyn turn the lock.

Her heart soared, her body thrummed. She'd never felt so loved and protected. Never felt as if she needed protecting, but she liked the new sensations he evoked in her. She snuggled in to him, trying to become one with him.

His touch mercuric, he lowered her to the bed, but the need for each other sent a wildfire through her. Animal instincts as old as time surfaced and dominated her thoughts and emotions. Touching the sleek skin of his torso, she lifted his shirt. He did the same to her. His fingers against her flesh burned with intensity. She tried to move closer.

In a matter of seconds, their clothes were on the floor, his naked body against hers. His hands roamed her length. He kissed her again, their lips melding, opening, and their tongues dueling each competing for supremacy, but she would not let him dominate, reveling in the feel of his body over hers, his strength and power so evident.

"God, Sugar, you're beautiful." He rose, straddling her then moved forward, closer, tracing her jawline, then down her neck. He followed with the tip of his tongue, stopping at her breasts, cupping them, teasing the nipple, rolling it between his fingers before kissing each one.

She didn't know how to respond to his words, except with a compliment to him as well. "Not as beautiful as you." She touched his chest, running a finger down the length then placed the palms of her hands on his abs. Muscle merged with muscle, a male specimen of rare beauty.

Her hips moved beneath him, telling him how much she needed him. His hand rested on her abdomen then he looked at her. His eyes seemed to speak from his soul as if she could read his mind. At that moment she knew, understood on the deepest level, he was her mate. They'd been together before, in another lifetime and they would be with each other now. Yolo, they say, you only live once, but it wasn't true, at least not for them. They had met and mated in other lifetimes. She wondered if others, normal people, had soul mates they searched for through eternity.

Then his lips closed over her nipple, tugging gently at first before he switched his attention to the other nipple, kissing his way down her length. She touched him, his broad back, felt his muscles ripple beneath her fingertips. His lips and tongue sketched a path down the inside of one leg, then up the other one, stopping briefly to place tender kisses behind her knee. She was hot and wet and ready for him, but it seemed he meant to torment her, prolong their lovemaking.

Needing him with desperate urgency, she tugged on him trying to tell him what she thought. But it didn't seem he wanted to hurry. He would do as he pleased when he pleased, yet everything he did inflamed her more, the fire growing, splintering within.

"Deacon, please..." her voice trailed off, her hips bucking as she proclaimed her need to feel all of him and to be one with her mate. "I need you now." Good Lord but she wanted to feel his length inside her, moving as one with her.

His hands and tongue roamed and touched. Hers followed suit yet he suddenly held her hands to her sides. "If you touch me, I'll explode."

"I don't want to stop, I don't want you to stop..."

"I need to love you, all of you," he told her, his fingers resting at the apex of her thighs, teasing, exploring. "You're very hot and wet." He slanted her a wicked grin. "You're pure sugar babe, pure sugar. My sweet talkin' sugar."

Beneath her ribs, her heart thundered. She wanted his cock inside her, filling her. But he didn't enter her. Instead his mouth covered her, his tongue delving inside. Her body shuddered and trembled her hips bucking wildly as she responded to him.

"Deacon, please..." Her mind spun. A haze of colors rippled through her head as she moved against him, needing him, wanting more from him. She thrust against him, spread her fingers through his hair, and frantically urged him closer. Her fingers closed around his shaft and she heard his response.

He groaned and sucked, licking, nipping, opening his mouth wide to cover her, he drove his tongue hard. She felt the spasms grow and finally her release came.

"Deacon!" she cried out as emotions overwhelmed her soul and her body wept with the mating.

He darted his tongue, in and out, while she ground against his mouth, and the ripples of her spasm spread from the apex of her thighs to encompass all of her.

Deacon slipped his hands beneath her ass and cupped her while she fell from the incredible high he'd brought her to, her body damp with sweat and weak from the exertion.

"Now you..." she told him. "It's your turn. I want to take you so high you will think you are soaring with the eagles."

He moved from her and padded into the living room, returning with a condom.

"Now me, now both of us, talk sweet to me, Sugar." In a matter of seconds he was deep inside her. She was ready for him. Her fingers toying with his male nipples while he plunged inside, slowly at first, and then harder and faster. She had no words, sweet or otherwise.

But just as she was about to reach the pinnacle and soar to the other side, he stopped.

"Deacon?" She was breathless.

"Hush, Sugar. I want this to be so good you'll never forget our first time." He didn't answer but bent over her and kissed the underside of her breast then ran his tongue around the aureole, stopping momentarily to lick and nip the tip. His hand slid down her body to reach inside her where she pulsed with need for him, finding her clit he touched it, massaged it bringing her once again to a pinnacle of desire.

Slowly he began to move, and she ignited, wildly bucking her hips against him, trying to bring him deeper inside. Her fingers digging into his back until she drew tiny droplets of blood.

He too, marked her flesh then drove deep and harder, together they became one. She screamed as the spasms overtook her and she let herself become part his world and his soul while he seemed to be absorbed into hers.

Spent, she lay beside him, spooned tightly together, and wishing this moment would never end. Closing her eyes and letting the earth spin, she waited for energy to fill her from within. Before she could speak, or think, he moved away then scooping her into his arms, carried her to the bathroom. Without putting her down, Deacon turned on the water slowly stepping inside with her and allowing her body to slide the length of his until her feet touched the tile below.

Every inch of his hard muscled body intrigued, fascinated, and drew her within to a point where she could no longer resist the pull that was Deacon McClain. He was hers and she was his. Dealing with this enchantment would be difficult if Deacon was not her soul mate. Fair enough, she would enjoy what he offered and when this was over, she'd find a way to explain why there couldn't be anything more between them. God, but she didn't think she could do that.

Lyn McKenna you're a fool if you think this man is not your mate. Yet, she couldn't dismiss that thought from her mind.

How on earth could she live without him? This wonderful man was inside her heart, as well as her soul. She knew the answer to her question.

"Deacon?" Her hands roved across his shoulders.

"Hmmm... Just don't stop what you're doing, Sugar, but what's on your mind?" He kissed her across her collarbone then up her neck to trace the shell of her ear with his tongue.

Keeping her hands running the length of his torso, reveling in the feeling of his hard abs beneath her fingertips was bliss. "I won't," her mind spun with simmering emotions. "Never."

Liquid warmth poured over her from above, and water jets on the side of the shower soothed aching muscles. Moments passed as she closed her eyes, absorbing the sensations of the moment.

Deacon pumped soap into his hands before lathering her body, following the curve of her hips then her belly. He turned her and pulled her against him, one hand holding her against him the other hand exploring her body.

"Have I told you how beautiful you are?" Letting the water rinse away the bubbles, he placed light kisses on her neck then across her collarbone.

"Not enough," she sighed, letting her head fall back against his chest, enjoying the moment.

"You are the most beautiful and intriguing woman I have ever met." Again, he turned her. "Wrap your legs around me."

She did as he asked. A moment later her back was against the tiled shower wall and he was inside her. The mating was fast and the climax explosive. She let a soft kiss bring her back to earth.

"You...you will be the death of me yet. My god, I swear I saw fireworks."

Deacon laughed and kissed her hard before opening the shower stall and grabbing a towel. He dried her off, tending to every inch of her body before patting her on the rear. "Time for bed. I want you curled up next to me for the entire night."

Over one shoulder, she slanted him what she thought was a flirtatious look before grabbing a shirt. "Ok."

"Leave it, the shirt. I forgot to tell you I wanted you naked."

"Don't you believe in asking?" she queried and slipped the shirt over her head. She heard a low growl then the shirt ripped and he scooped her into his arms. Together, they fell onto the bed.

A little while later, Deacon pushed away from Lyn then picked up his ringing phone. He bent over and kissed her on the nose. Lyn pulled the sheets to her breasts, covering herself and watched him. He walked to the bedroom door and peeked out then turned his attention back to the phone.

"It's on speaker," he said and walked back to the bed, setting it on the sheets as he sat down.

"Hey, little sis, how are you?"

Lyn felt heat rise to her cheeks, thinking about just how fine she was after making love with Deacon. She swallowed and said, "Good. How are you?"

The laughter on the other end was a bit unnerving. "Just letting you know, we are about to intercept Balor. You should be safe from the demon soon. I reckon you'll be able to come home tomorrow or the next day."

"Uh... I don't think so." Lyn looked to Deacon.

"I don't like the way that sounds," Brody told her, his voice harsh.

"Don't threaten me. Deacon and I have some things we have to take care of here before we can go home."

"What things?" Brody queried.

Lyn looked to Deacon for answers but his easy grin was maddening. She knew he wasn't going to help her with an explanation. His shrug solidified her thoughts.

She shot him a look she hoped sent daggers his way. "We want to do some sight seeing. Chat with the locals we've met." She knew she was hedging and guessed Brody would see right through her lie.

"And..."

"And," Deacon interrupted, "we won't give you all the details but there is nothing dangerous about what we've planned. We love Nafplio and would like to explore the countryside when we don't have a demonic threat hanging over our heads."

"I see..."

But the ensuing pause told Lyn her brother didn't understand anything, but he was trying, which was unlike Brody. She expected him to give the ultimatum *come home now or I'm coming to get you.*

"We will stay in touch. By the way, do you know what time it is over here?" Deacon said.

"You picked up the phone. I expected to leave a message so it must be day, or..."

Again Lyn didn't care for the pause or the silent thoughts coming from the other end of the phone.

"It's the middle of the night," Deacon began. "We couldn't sleep so we went out for food. We need some sleep so I think I'll let you and your brothers fight the demon, and Lyn and I will get some much needed shuteye." He punched the end the phone call button.

Lyn inhaled a quick gasp of air, wishing Deacon hadn't implied what she thought he'd just implied and what she was sure her brother would believe. "That wasn't too politically correct."

"But it's the truth. Your brother doesn't need to know we've found each other. If he did know, however, he would be happy for you."

"You don't think he'd grab the family jet and head to Nafplio? I do."

"He wouldn't. Brody knows you're of age and he's already guessed our feelings for each other."

"I'm not ready to plan a wedding." Lyn crossed her arms and stared hard at Deacon whose lazy grin once again maddened her. "It's not funny." She threw a pillow at him, losing the sheet she held in front of her.

He tackled her, wrapping his arms around her. "You're fuckin' beautiful, woman." He told her as his lips found a nipple and tugged.

"Again," Lyn queried. "I'm exhausted."

"Better find energy because I want you now and I really don't want to take no for an answer."

"I need sleep." But she knew the movement of her hips searching for contact with his gave credence to her lie. "Yes," she told him, "I lied. I want you more now than I did the first time."

"When we're done here," he told her as he trailed kisses down her neck and across the collarbone. All he had to do was look at her with his sexy and too gorgeous baby blue eyes and she melted.

"I want to sleep sometime tonight," she protested once more even though she didn't want him to stop.

"Of course you do," he moved down her body, touching, exploring every inch.

"But..." her hips bucked when his lips found her core. She had no more energy and it seemed neither did he.

~ * ~

"What do you want to do today?" Deacon looked over his shoulder at his woman as he washed the glasses from the night before. If he could have his way, they would spend all day and all night in bed.

"Catch us some poachers and go home." Lyn padded to where he stood and kissed his cheek. "Good morning."

"Good morning to you." He brushed hair from her face, and cupping it in his hands, he kissed her on the lips then backed away to watch her. He loved looking at her, was starved to spend more alone time with her, quality moments they'd remember forever.

She put a piece of bread in the toaster then leaned back on the counter. "We have to wait for Jonathan to call, don't we?"

"We do. I think the best course of action is to act like tourists and go shopping. The stores hold lots of interesting objects, clothing, jewelry, paintings and more." He waggled his eyebrows at her and it was all he could do to keep himself from laughing at her expression.

"We are tourists." Lyn popped up the bread, looked at it, grimaced then sent it back for more toasting. "We don't have to act, but shopping sounds like fun. Only problem is that I don't have money or a credit card."

"You like to shop? Then you can use my card and you can pay me back later." Deacon set the last glass on the dish drainer, knowing he'd said the latter part just in time to keep her protest at bay.

"Of course I like to shop." She shrugged. "Don't have any money or my credit or debit cards," she reiterated, saying the words with emphasis this time, "and I won't use yours."

"I have money." He needed to tread carefully. She'd just admitted he was the one, but she was fiercely independent too.

"I don't want your money." She popped up the toast before walking outside to sit and eat.

He followed, not wanting to second-guess her stiff shoulders and matter-of-fact stride to the terrace. "Consider it a loan. After all, I didn't give you a chance to grab anything, before we started our whirlwind expedition."

She paused for several long seconds. To Deacon the time seemed an eternity. "I'll have to think about it. Right now I need caffeine and a hot shower—by myself." She did slant him a smile which looked sexy as hell.

He laughed from deep inside and the sound rolled out. "Done." He really didn't know why. Respecting her privacy was important even though a shower with her sounded inviting. "I'll get breakfast. Something more satisfying than toast and coffee."

"It's a deal. Where are you going?" she asked, looking over her shoulder as she walked to the bedroom.

"The rooftop. They serve breakfast until ten o'clock and if I get going, I'll just have time to pick up a few things to eat. Anything special?" he queried, wishing he knew her so well he didn't have to ask.

"No, I like just about anything. You can choose for me." With that said Lyn disappeared into the bedroom.

Deacon closed his eyes, his imagination working overtime. Damn, he could envision every sweet curve of her body. Groaning, he slipped his wallet and phone into his pocket and left the room, locking the door behind him then inhaled two long deep breaths of air.

Taking the steps two at a time, he ran to the top of the building. He was greeted by a server. Giving his and Lyn's name to her, he explained how he was taking breakfast to the room.

She nodded to the trays of food. Deacon picked up a tray, a couple of plates and two cups of coffee then he browsed the line. Greek yogurt accompanied by honey, tomatoes and cucumbers, eggs and ham and of course more toast.

His stomach growled. He grinned at the lady, keeping tabs on the guest. "I'll bring these back. Promise."

She shook her head and told him to leave the trays outside their room and the maids would take care of them.

When he returned, he could hear the shower turn off and he guessed Lyn was stepping from the stall—naked. Keeping his randy mind away from thoughts of sex with his girl was not easy, but he was determined not to make their early relationship just about sex.

A few minutes later Lyn stepped from the room, dressed in walking shorts and a little pink top. "Hmm...smells good."

"I think I took a little of everything." He handed her a cup of coffee then stepped away so she could have first pick of the food he brought.

She filled her plate then walked outside to sit. He followed. They ate in silence. He wanted to know her every thought, but again, needed to give her privacy. He wished he could read her mind and hoped some day he could second-guess everything she thought, wanted or needed.

"I'm finished," she said as she leaned back, her hand resting on the handle of her coffee cup.

"Me too." He rose and, taking the plates and the tray, set them outside their door. "We can wash the cups and use them tomorrow."

"I'm looking forward to shopping even though I technically don't have any money."

"I'm going to ask for every cent back," he told her although he didn't mean a word of what he'd just said. If she didn't remember to pay him back when she had the funds, he wasn't going to remind her. He wanted to pamper her and buy her everything and anything she wanted.

"Come on," she said, "I made a mental list of who I want to purchase something for and," she paused, "we have our work cut out for us. I'm kind of hoping Jonathan doesn't call."

With a quick step and a flirtatious look that had him wanting to scoop her into his arms and take her to bed, she stepped through the door. "Bring it on, I'll be your pack horse."

"Really?"

"Yup."

"First, I'm going to find a purse." She skipped down the steps to the front of the hotel and out the door before looking over her shoulder. "I've really missed not having a purse and lipstick and mascara, and..." she paused, "just about everything."

He followed, enjoying the day and easy camaraderie between them. He felt at home and at ease with Lyn. This was the way the rest of his life would be. *Their* lives would be, he corrected himself.

They walked along the narrow streets. Dogs lay on the sidewalk and watched them with sleepy lidded eyes. A few natives stopped to pet the animals, but for the most part the people left them alone to take their morning naps.

Lyn walked into a linen shop and bought table runners and place mats, shaking her head and looking at him as if he lacked inspiration.

"I need a purse." She left the little shop and set off down the street. "I can find bags and scarves and key chains, but no purses." Deacon heard her mutter. He'd fix this if he could, but it didn't seem prudent to search elsewhere, knowing he needed to stay with her.

"When you find one, a purse, what are you going to put in it?" he queried.

"Just like a man," she told him. "Didn't I just make a list? You weren't listening, were you? I heard on a talk show that men only listen to a woman for three minutes. When I find one, a purse not a man, I'm going to buy a wallet and put it in the purse then I'm going to buy lipstick and..."

"There's a purse shop."

She walked in and looked around, finally settling on a small purse with a long strap, one he assumed could be put over a shoulder then draped across her front for safety.

At the counter, she stopped then looked at him grimacing. "I need..."

He swore under his breath at his insensitivity and stepped up, bringing his wallet from his pocket and pulling out his credit card. He watched the gorgeous blush sweep up her cheeks but regretted the fact.

The clerk accepted his card and ran the transaction, saying, "Do you want it wrapped?"

Lyn shook her head and the man handed it to her. "Thank you, have a good day."

"You too," the clerk told her. "Have a nice day."

A jewelry store around the corner beckoned and Lyn spent a while looking at earrings, buying two pairs plus a ring for Kimi.

Deacon's phone rang. He looked at Lyn, "I have to take this." She slanted him a quizzical look, "It's my dad." He needed to hear from his father, but he really didn't like having this time interrupted.

She nodded, "Sean?"

"Yes," he told her as he watched her return to shopping.

"What is it?" Deacon asked.

"Just wanted to let you know I've arrived in Cactus Junction. The brother's are chasing after Balor, but I assume you know this."

"Yes, Brody called to let me know. What's your assessment?" His gut tightened, fear for Lyn rose to the forefront of his mind.

"I'm not sure. I've only been here a little while. I haven't met the McKennas. Right now, I'm on my way to the ranch just south of town. It seems they own most of Cactus Junction."

"Yup, that was my assessment too." It didn't matter to him who owned what. He knew his family owned many acres of land in Ireland and near Yosemite in the US. He just wanted Lyn to be safe and happy and to live the rest of her life with him.

"What do you want me to do?" Sean's tense voice came through the phone.

"Just introduce yourself to the family. Kimi knows who I am and that I'm with Lyn. I assume Brody and Carr have told the family the rest of the story."

"All right, I'll get back to you then." His father hung up the phone.

"See you soon," Deacon said after the fact, then slipped the phone into his pocket and looked for Lyn. She stood just inside a small store, her back to him.

He walked to her and put his arms around her, pulling her close. He felt her little gasp of surprise and heard the following sigh of pleasure. "Um... don't tell my boyfriend."

"I won't," he whispered close to her ear before kissing the lobe and wishing he could kiss more of her.

She leaned into him as he ran his hands upward, stopping when he remembered just where they were. In his arms, she turned. Looking at him with her gorgeous blue eyes and feeling her body fit precisely next to his, his thoughts turned sexual. Just as he closed his eyes, deciding to step back, her lips were on his and her tongue in his mouth.

He reciprocated the kiss, reveling in the fire racing inside and the need to sweep her into his arms and carry her back to the room.

The sound of a man clearing his throat behind him brought him back to the present and doused the flames burning through his body.

"Don't let me interrupt."

"Jonathan. Your timing's off."

"Sorry. Thought you would want to know another trap was found just west of here."

With that bit of information, Jonathan left.

"What, why?" Lyn's hands were on her hips. "I don't get it. He just stopped to give us the news then leaves."

"He can't risk anyone seeing us together." Deacon wondered about that too, and it was the only plausible explanation for his behavior. But the poachers didn't know who they were. "Does Jonathan want us to investigate this?"

Lyn's quizzical look made him laugh.

"You're still not making sense. I don't know why he'd ask that."

"I know. I'm just trying to figure it out too. Let's finish shopping and grab a bite to eat.

She paused, her hand on his shoulder. "You know, I'm not really hungry. I've been eating so much, I probably need to stop."

"You mean quit eating?"

"I...well, I don't want to get fat."

"You're not fat and even if you were, I'd love you just as much." Deacon didn't know where this conversation was going. He'd seen her toying with her food from time to time and pushing it around on her plate and he remembered her telling him about her anorexia but...

A wild scream emanating from the fortress of Bourtzi in the bay riffled the air, stopping all where they stood.

Deacon's heart raced with constricting fear, and he felt Lyn move against him, putting her hands on his arms. The trembling in her hands terrified and filled his mind with dread.

~ * ~

Hot sun battered the over-dry earth. Rain hadn't fallen in weeks and parts of the Sierra Madres were on fire. Smoke from a nearby fire filled the air and coated Brody's lungs. Damn. But he hoped this would be over soon. He needed clean air as well as closure to this evil demon who threatened his family. Lyn needed to come home and sort out her feelings for Deacon McClain.

"Where was Balor sighted?" Carr asked as he disrobed and stacked his clothes by a tree.

"Near the caves," came the answer from Brody.

"The hot springs?" Carr shifted into his cat form.

"You can't wait to get going, little brother, not even for an answer?" Brody looked at the skyline and the mountains of the Sierra Madres. He had a bad feeling, one he prayed he wouldn't regret.

Carr let out a wild scream. Angel had shifted too, his howl accompanied the screech.

"The hot springs where..." Brody didn't want to mention how he'd spent those nights with Sadie so he was relieved Balor had been sighted at the creepy hole in the rocks they'd been warned to stay away from as kids.

Apache legend told of strange happenings in the cave, supernatural events. Mothers had warned that if they ventured into the cave, they would never be seen again.

Of course as children they'd believed the stories told by their mothers, but there were also tales told around the campfire at night when the fire burned low and a full moon hung in the sky.

He cleared his throat realizing he hadn't yet told them about the cave. "It's crystal cave." Then he waited for a reaction.

Carr let out another scream. Brody didn't think Angel would have heard about this place, but an ensuing growl told him different. "I know. We'll have to be careful. If we end up some place else, I want us all to be in Nafplio when our feet touch ground. So—we think of Nafplio—agreed?"

The pair nodded, then as if in unison they sat, waiting for Brody to shift.

Brody shifted then led the way. The speed he set was an easy lope. They had ridden to an area close to the caves. A mile only separated them from the tethered horses and the hole in the wall called Crystal Springs. Brody couldn't hold back a small grin when they passed the hot springs cave, remembering every precious moment of his time spent with Sadie.

I'm going to bring her back.

At the entrance of the next cave the trio stopped, waiting. Brody inhaled a few deep breaths. The distance hadn't been far and they covered it in less than twelve minutes. Yet he and Carr were built for speed, not distance and he didn't want to risk their lives by going inside too soon. They were both spent and they needed a moment to regain their composure and thoughts.

Inside, blackness enveloped them. For a brief moment, Brody's heart stopped and he couldn't breathe. This place felt evil. The three padded softly through the darkness. Further into the cave the heat—the heat became unbearable. Sweat poured from Brody.

Baylor?

Brody saw him about one hundred feet away. Staggering through the cave, he looked drunk. It was the only word Brody could think of to describe his movements. Deeper into the cave, they continued walking, moving ever deeper, fear knew real terror and he felt the old legends seep into his head.

This was a place of fear and they'd ventured into it. Brody knew retreat was not an option. He looked to his brother and Angel. Even in their shifter forms, he saw the grim resignation but knew they would follow.

A deep breath filled his lungs and he moved forward, motioning with his head for the others to continue. Dread, fear, apprehension were all real thoughts, but excitement also raced through him. He needed to understand the complexities of this cave and he knew this place was not all evil.

Strange things happened here. Maybe people disappeared but it wasn't all bad.

Balor staggered through the tunnel. A strange light shown down on him, highlighting his form, then he vanished.

Brody heard the others inhale air. They'd seen the apparition too. Looking at them, he nodded in the direction where Baylor had vanished. Brody didn't know why but he guessed this had to do with Lyn. They had to follow, risk their lives, and see what...?

Chapter Seven

Shock waves whipped through Lyn, her gaze focused on the island of Bourtzi. The air around the fortress sparkled with light and a red glow emanated around the building. The night sky appeared filled with fireworks and explosions reverberated in the air.

"What is it?" Her heart raced with fear and she placed her hand on her chest. "Whatever it is, it can't be good.

"I don't think I care to learn," Deacon moved closer to the bay, shielding his eyes from the blinding lights.

Out of the sparks flying through the sky and mirrored across the bay, a silhouette of a large body stumbled from the fort and into the water. With strong sure strokes, the form made it's way toward the mainland.

A shiver of distress landed in the pit of her stomach as she held her breath and closed her eyes for a moment. "It's Balor, isn't it? He's found us." She swallowed hard before clearing her throat.

"Don't jump to conclusions." Deacon's words gave warning but did nothing to build her confidence or ease the terror.

"Shit! Don't jump to conclusions?" Lyn parroted. "What are we going to do? I know it's him. It's too spooky to be anything but supernatural. And that man..." she pointed toward the swimmer.

"We are going to go back to our room. He won't know where to find you and we're going to figure this out."

Panic struck. "That's what you told me when we teleported here." She turned, but another flash of light flared from the island, catching her attention. More fireworks and explosions scorched the Greek countryside. Terror shot down her spine.

People gathered in the parking lot across from the fort, chattering about the phenomenon. From all sides she heard, "what the fuck," and gasps of inhaled breaths as every one stared out to sea.

Out of the smoke now encasing the fortress, loped two jaguars and a huge wolf. "Oh, my God." Lyn clung to Deacon's arm, hoping the contact would keep her from fainting. "Oh, my God." The sight gave credence to the fact the first man they'd seen was the demon Balor.

"Your brothers?" Deacon queried. "Who's the wolf?"

"Angel. Angel McKenna." She spoke in a hushed tone as she stared at the water. Balor swam in front of the McKennas, but the scene brought a hush to the waterfront. The calm settling over Lyn was timeless, feeling as if it lasted an eternity when in reality the peace had lasted a millisecond.

"McKenna Clan? Really? And a wolf?"

"Yeah, I'll explain later. We've got to help them. They won't have any clothes and they won't know where to find us." Her panic had turned into action, her fear for herself into fear for her family, yet she stood frozen to the concrete.

"Yeah, yeah, I... You go back to the condo. Get pants at least. Hope mine will fit, maybe a pair of shorts for the wolf. I think he's bigger than the others. I'll meet you in the east woods, just on the edge."

For another moment, she couldn't will her feet to move, then Deacon's words caught hold in her mind and she raced through the milling crowd mindless of the people she hit in her mad dash. Stumbling once on uneven pavement, her arms whirling in huge circles, she stopped her fall. Hand to her chest, she paused, bent over, heaving air.

When she looked up, her condo was feet away. Not wanting to call attention to herself, she walked quickly to the main door, and as she passed the clerk, she nodded then took the steps two at a time.

Hurry, hurry.

Once inside, she rummaged through Deacon's clothes, finding two pair of jeans and elastic waist shorts.

I hope these fit them.

Can it be too much to ask or wonder how Balor and her brothers and cousin arrived in Nafplio at the same time and place? And they came through the fort on the island? How?

Ten minutes later she reached the edge of the east woods, as they called it. She wasn't sure if she should call out or let them find her, but if her brothers were naked, that was a picture she didn't want to see.

For a few seconds, clothes in her arms she turned in circles, waiting for a clue as to their whereabouts. Thoughts of the poachers finding them swept through her head. Then thoughts of Jonathan and members of his clan came to mind. More damage might be done this night. Everyone around the cafés had seen the animals.

"Deacon," she whispered. "Where are you guys? Is everything all right?" Her heart in her throat, she whirled in another circle.

"Over here." Deacon strode down a trail. "I had to move them deeper into the woods. With all of the people watching the bay, it was hard to catch up to them. Needless to say, Jonathan isn't going to be happy when he hears about the sightings."

"I don't care about Jonathan right now. Are they okay? Did they tell you what happened?"

"Not yet. They've stayed in their shifter form until clothes arrived. Didn't want to get caught naked."

"Yeah, that would be a bit too vulnerable. Here," Lyn handed the clothes to Deacon. "Go do what you need to do. I'll be fine."

Deacon looked from the forest to Lyn. "I..."

"I'll wait here and I'll yell my head off if I see the demon. After that I'll run as fast as I can to you, naked brothers and cousin or not."

Deacon hesitated again. "Promise."

"Cross my heart," she told him. "Now hurry. I want to get them all home and find out what happened."

Without further comment, Deacon ran into the woods.

Lyn crossed her arms over her chest, a chill rifling her body. *What's taking them so long?* She paced down the trail then back up again. A breeze whistled around her, night sounds she would have normally loved sent fear through her body and set her nerves on edge. An owl hooted in the night, but she didn't feel as if it brought her luck. The sun slithered behind a cloud, casting the woods in darkness.

"Sis." Brody sauntered from the woods. Carr, Angel and Deacon following him as if they were little ducks in a row.

At that moment the moon decided to reveal itself again. Warmth and a sensation of safety filled her.

"Good to see you. Now, let's get out of this place and home so you can tell us what happened."

Good to see..." Brody began

"Have you seen Balor?" Angel interrupted the conversation between the siblings as he peered down the trail.

"I haven't, but I doubt he's going to show himself in the village." Lyn linked her arm through Brody's and kept pace with him.

"No, don't suppose he will." But that didn't keep Carr from peering down the trail.

Lyn looked over her shoulder at Angel. "How did you get messed up in this? Nice shorts."

Angel ran his hands through his hair, "They're a little tight but I guess they'll have to do until I can shop. And how I got involved you ask? Well, it seems Phaedra wanted to visit Margo and I came with her. I volunteered, and they, your brothers, didn't turn me down. The rest speaks for itself."

"And you can't resist an adventure or what might be over the hill." Lyn laughed.

"Nope, but none of us really expected to end up in Greece." Carr said. "When we stepped inside Crystal Cave, no one believing the stories Grandfather used to tell.

"You didn't." At the mention of the cave a cold sweat broke out on Lyn's body. "I've always believed those stories. Every time I've been close, my gut told me to run as far away as I could."

"I thought Grandfather told them to scare us into behaving. It always seemed he threatened us with dire circumstances and trip to some unknown place if we didn't do what the elders said." Carr laughed, "I guess I was wrong. The tales were true."

Walking along the edge of the forest with the others gave Lyn a feeling of security. She didn't know where Balor was and knew they would have to find him, but that was for another time. The fifteen-minute journey back to the condo passed in silence.

On their trip to the apartment, they stopped for food and clothes. Angel looked relieved when he found jeans and a couple of shirts that would fit.

Thoughts of their crazy ride from the Sierra Madres filled her head. Lyn wanted to hear every detail. They stopped at the hotel desk to see if there were rooms for travelers. Brody booked a room down the hall from Lyn's and Deacon's. Lyn expected her brother to tell her she would have to stay with them, but he didn't.

Once settled and inside, they mingled, chatting about nonsensical and unimportant things until Lyn finished opening boxes of take out and pouring drinks. Once the plates and silverware were piled high with the food, everyone helped themselves to the bounty. After settling on the chairs around the living room table, the real conversation began.

Between bites, Lyn said, "Start from the beginning. I want to hear every last detail."

Brody sipped his beer, staring outside for a moment before he cleared his throat and began the tale. "We left the ranch with the horses in the trailer behind the truck. We didn't think we'd have to go very far before we caught up to Balor and scare the livin' crap out of him."

"But we lost him," Carr interjected.

"And we lost time when Carr and Brody started arguing about the best way to find him," Angel grinned then bit into his hamburger.

"We weren't arguing," Brody said.

"What would you call it then?" Angel asked.

"A debate? A conversation?" Carr said.

"Just like you two to spend too much time trying to figure out a plan and losing the desired object in the process. Seems something like that happened with your quest to catch the Amazonian Devil. You ended up going the wrong way and had to double back."

Brody groaned. "I don't like to think about that day. I nearly lost my wife and you."

"But you didn't," Angel reminded them. "Where do you all think Balor is?"

"He's got to be lurking somewhere." Brody picked up a French fry dipping it in Tzatziki sauce before eating it.

"I'm sure he's hungry and cold. Our guys who were following him said he hadn't eaten in a couple of days. He managed to get some water in him when he passed over the creek meandering by the cave," Carr said.

Lyn smiled, looking from brother to brother. "So, go on with the story. What happened when you watched him go into the cave?"

"How do you know we saw him?" Carr asked.

"If you didn't see him, you would have never ventured inside. I know you guys. Even though you say you aren't superstitious and never believed the tales weren't true, you two have always given that place distance. I've been on enough trips to Grandfather's home to know."

"You're right as usual, Lyn," Brody continued. "We reached the mouth and held back for a few seconds. I'm not sure we would have followed if Angel hadn't been there."

"Me?"

"Yeah, neither one of us wanted to admit we were fuckin' scared." Carr laughed. "But we were."

"Inside the air was foul and very little light filtered through the cracks in the thick rock. Our cat eyes were able to see better than if we'd been in human form. Still, I'd wished for a flashlight."

"I'm the smart one," Carr said, as he swirled the wine in his glass before sipping.

"Yeah right," Brody muttered. "It was only a few seconds before we saw Balor standing in a circle of light. The light filtered in a cone-like shape from the ceiling. Balor stumbled on the rocks, staggering as if he were drunk and repeating the word 'rip'."

"What did he mean by that?" Lyn stood, stretching her back and legs, wishing she could relax, but with her brothers here and the tension with Balor so close the tightness settled between her shoulders. She looked at Brody for an answer, "Rip?"

"Don't know but a few seconds later, a loud noise shook the cave and he disappeared," Brody said.

"Mindless of the danger, all three of us rushed to the spot where he'd been standing seconds earlier. The light had vanished, leaving us in the darkness except for the tiny beam emanating from Carr's flashlight."

"Everything you're saying gives me chills." Lyn rubbed her arms to rid herself of the goose bumps.

"Me too," Angel said. "To hear your brothers tell the story seems a lot scarier than when it happened. A few seconds after Balor vanished, the light encircled us. I had time to say one word before we were whisked from the cave just as Baylor had been moments earlier."

~ * ~

Deacon had been quiet, seeming to listen to the story. "And what was that word?"

"Can't say it in the presence of a lady," Angel muttered looking away for a moment.

"You were supposed to be thinking Nafplio." Carr told him.

"I had you two to do that for me. I didn't want to think of anywhere. Wanted to stay right where I was."

"I get it, but we had to follow the demon," Carr said.

"And...it's a good thing we did," Brody added.

"What now?" Lyn brushed a wayward strand of hair from her face before crinkling her brows as if in concentration. "Do we run again? I'm sure Deacon can teleport me anywhere, but I don't want to go."

"We go after Baylor." Deacon wished there was another way, had truly hoped Lyn's brothers would have vanquished him while they were still in the Sierra Madres. He'd always understood Balor's demise wouldn't be easy.

"Tomorrow, first light," Brody said. "Everyone agreed?"

"Agreed," was the murmur around the room.

Brody stood. "Let's clean up the dishes and take-out, then go to our rooms. I think these two need some alone time."

Deacon wasn't sure what to make of that comment, but agreed. "Thanks." His mind spun with the ramifications. He knew Lyn cared about him but was also sure she wasn't ready to call him her beloved for life—through eternity and all of that.

With the chores finished, the brothers and Angel were ready to leave. Brody gave Lyn a quick kiss on one cheek as did Carr. Then the door closed behind the men. Silence for a moment sent an eerie feeling through him.

Deacon's sigh of relief echoed in the near empty room.

Lyn laughed. "You felt the tension too?" She downed her glass of wine then poured another.

"Crap, two of your brothers and a cousin? I thought they'd make sure, with their fists, that I would treat you right."

"And they didn't even ask me to join them. I'd say they're pretty understanding guys." She winked flirtatiously at him.

Deacon groaned, "They know you're my partner forever, and they would never stand between us."

"How do they know all of this if I don't?" She leaned against the sliding glass door to the balcony, cocking her head to one side, seeming to stare into the night.

To Deacon, she appeared to need answers he wasn't ready to give and she wasn't ready to hear. He shrugged though, believing Lyn needed at least one answer. "The marks on your shoulder."

"What?" She looked at her arm moving it forward so she could see what he alluded. "It's scratched."

"More than that." Deacon loved the way her eyes shimmered when she was curious.

"I don't get it." She looked at her other shoulder. "Just scratches. Does that mean something?"

118

Fuck. "It told your clan two things. We've slept together and you are my mate. Those marks would not be there if what I just said wasn't true."

Lyn's face turned ashen. Without a word she sat down, her wine spilling on the floor in tiny burgundy droplets.

Deacon paced. Back and forth. The room felt too small. Seconds turned into minutes. He stared at Lyn then paced. Needing fresh air, he stepped to the balcony.

Unexpectedly, she was beside him. "I can't deny the facts." Lyn stood beside him, her hand on his forearm, stopping him. "You're my mate then. What do we do now?"

Relieved at her acceptance, Deacon wiped away the sweat beading on his forehead. "You are mine and I am yours." His tone measured and hesitant, he waited for her reaction.

"Good, I'm glad to know for sure. From the first time I met you, I thought maybe…but all the myths confused me. I felt so many things for you, but nothing like the way I thought I was supposed to feel."

The grin spreading across his face grew. "Me too."

"The emotions seem to go soul deep; my love growing with each passing second but we've had such fear to deal with. I didn't want to confuse my need for your protection with love." Lyn ran her hand up his arm then back, sending goose bumps running throughout.

Deacon's cell rang. "It's Jonathan."

"Why aren't I surprised?"

"Hello, I'm putting us on speaker."

"What the hell happened? More shifters. The poachers will never leave and they will always be a threat. You have to fix this."

Deacon cleared his throat, trying to decide on the best choice of words. "Lyn's brothers fell through a void called Crystal Springs cave in the Sierra Madres. They were chasing the demon who is after Lyn."

"As shifters?" The doubt in Jonathan's voice was evident. "Why the hell did they shift? It wouldn't have been a problem for us if they'd arrived in human form."

"It was the best way to chase and scare Baylor."

"How the fu—did it happen? One just doesn't move from point A to point B without something supernatural happening."

"It seems the McKenna Clan knows how to use a cave to their advantage."

"Well, technically Baylor started it," Lyn added.

"I don't understand. You know the jeopardy this places on the shifters who live here? The poachers saw your jaguar brothers and the wolf. Who is that wolf by the way?"

"Angel, my cousin," Lyn told Jonathan and whoever was listening. "No one is really sure why there is branch of our family who are wolf shifters, but there seem to be."

"You did tell them the problem we have?" Jonathan's voice broke with the question.

"Not yet."

"Why the hell not?"

From the background, Deacon heard a smashing object and a shriek he assumed was Cherise.

"We had more pressing matters," Deacon tried to stay calm, a difficult task when it was Lyn's life that was in danger.

"What could be more important than the lives of all who live here in Nafplio?"

Once again, Deacon tried to retain a quiet air of calm while his gut churned. "Baylor, the demon who arrived first has been sent to bring Lyn to Ireland as a sacrifice." Deacon told Jonathan the story, leaving out no details.

"All right. I concede. If Cherise's life were in danger, I would do the same."

"Glad you understand. Listen," Deacon paced the small room. "We plan on venturing into the forest tomorrow, first light."

"In your human form." Jonathan stated.

"Of course." Outraged that Jonathan would think anything different, Deacon said. "You think we're stupid?"

"No, no, just making sure we're thinking the same way." The tone in Jonathan's voice seemed to apologize without saying the words.

"Good, we hope to find Baylor and end the threat. After that we can deal with the poachers. I promise you no one will shift unless the circumstance is dire."

"I don't like the sound of that."

Deacon looked to Lyn who seemed unfazed by the conversation. She smiled at him, seeming lost in her thoughts. He wanted to know what was going on in her head then he wanted to take her to bed. Sex with his Lyn was magnificent, but distracting. With Baylor on the loose in Nafplio, he couldn't be distracted.

The sound piercing the night air sent shudders through his body.

~ * ~

Baylor wiped sweat from his forehead, his belly churning. His breath had been stolen from him when the white light sucked him through a pitch-black void. He'd landed hard on an island. Not knowing where he was he stumbled through a maze of smoke and shimmering lights to fall into seawater.

Seawater of all things.

"Rip, rip..." he was back where he'd come from. The sea demons had called to him. They would kill him because he'd failed and he would rest now. Sleep seemed so wonderful, the thought exciting him. He couldn't remember when he'd rested, slept in a peaceful bliss. It had been so long, so very long.

Tepid ocean washed over him as he swam. Feelings of bliss swept through him and reminders of a past he'd thought forgotten. This ocean was unlike that of the Celtic Sea and the locks in Scotland. This water was warm, filled with bliss. What better place to meet his fate.

I could get used to this.

His breath caught in his throat and he swallowed water. Choking, he spit the liquid drops burning inside his nose.

I'm getting old.

Land appeared far distant. His strokes grew choppy and seconds turned into minutes. He grew tired and thought to stop swimming so he could slip beneath the water.

Rip, rip, rip...

He closed his eyes; a slow rhythm came to him as if thousands of years hadn't passed. He knew if he set his mind, he could make it. When his lids fluttered open, the land was near. More strokes, more water lapping over his head, then his knee hit ground.

He jerked and his heart leapt to his throat. But the real land was still ahead of him. This was a false alarm, just like everything else that had happened to him since his rise from the dead. Nothing was as it seemed.

Minutes later he stood on solid ground. People swarmed around him. He looked one way then the other.

"Get out of my way..." he waved his hands motioning for them to move. They parted as he barged through them, growling. The third eye he always kept closed, opened. Before he could close it, one man fell dead.

"Out..."

The voices surrounding him spoke gibberish. He didn't understand what anyone said. "No!"

Trees stretched in front of him. He ran, bushes and low lying branches scratched him and tore at his clothes. When he turned to look over his shoulder, he saw no one.

Winded, legs aching from the exertion he leaned against a tree and slowly lowered himself to a sitting position. Tears welled in his throat then seeped from his eyes. He cried, letting all of the tension and fear release.

Hours later, his stomach grumbling, the moon hanging in the sky and stars twinkling, he rose. Food now was his first thought; he stumbled toward the small town of Nafplio.

Why is there never any food where I'm sent?

Seeking the alleys, he looked in dumpsters to find parts of left over meals. He didn't know what he ate, just that his stomach was no longer hollow. Beside him a dog growled, baring his teeth.

Christine Young

Balor thought to kick the dog away, but realized the animal was just as hungry. He held out a small piece of bread. The dog snatched it from his hand, swallowing it in a gulp.

He grabbed a bottle of beer from behind a cardboard box and found it still held liquid. The beer didn't quench his thirst. The seawater had taken its toll.

A few yards down the alley a man stepped from the kitchen of a restaurant, scrapping scraps of food onto the walkway. One yellow dog rose from nearby and sauntered to the food as if he were king. Other dogs along the alley watched as if indifferent.

Balor needed more food. But for some unknown reason he understood these scraps were for this dog. They each seemed to have their own territory.

The need for clothes and food gave him courage. Staying in the shadows and trying not to draw attention to himself, he found a clothing store still open, a woman outside, trying to beckon tourists inside. When she wasn't looking, he grabbed a t-shirt from a pile lying by the opening and backed into a corner. Ripping the tags off, he slipped out of the old shirt and into the new one.

His belly slightly filled and wearing a clean shirt, rest was next on his list. He needed to think this through and figure out what to do next. All he really wanted was to return to his country and find solace in death. He wanted nothing more than to rest in peace. Living was not what he'd expected.

R.I.P.

The dark forest terrified him. An owl's hoot sent shivers down his spine. Sweat spilled from his armpits and down his back. He liked the Irish Sea and the cool weather.

Shielding his eyes, he searched for the trail. Nothing. The lump in his throat grew. Even the chirping of some animal scared him. Maybe they'd scare him to death.

One could only pray.

In this land and this time, he didn't know who or what god to pray to. Scrubbing his face with his hands, he stumbled into a thicket. All he wanted

123

right now was to find a sweet place to sleep. Possibilities of not waking up simmered inside.

His eyes closed and hoping his wishes would come true, he waited for that sweet moment.

Nothing.

God, what did he need to do? His mind was made up but he didn't have the strength to take his life. He couldn't.

Thoughts of his children came to him in a bliss filled mist. He saw their little faces, at least the way he remembered them. Where were they now? Where was the grandson who killed him?

R.I.P.

What he'd wished for and bargained for had gone against the natural way of life. No wonder he was living this hell. What had he done?

Started something unnatural, that's what he'd done. Now he had to make everything right, beg someone to kill him.

The McKennas would do that, murder him. But he didn't want them to suffer for their crime. No, he needed a plan.

Suddenly, the pain was excruciating.... he let out a yell, a never-ending scream then fell to the earth.

Chapter Eight

A shadow knifed through Lyn's heart at the excruciating sound ripping apart the night air. Chills slithered snake-like down her body, her feet frozen to the ground.

White knuckled, her hands gripped the balcony railing. Then she turned to Deacon who stood with hands clenched at his sides, his expression grim.

"What in God's name was that?" Lyn blurted the question, knowing Deacon would not have an answer.

She watched his jaw clench. "I don't know." Yet he stepped forward, reaching out to her and pulling her inside, then holding her close for a moment.

Pushing away from him, she peered over the railing and searched the darkness for answers. "It sounded human. That was the same type of sound I heard when Balor was thrown from the fort. Wasn't it?"

"Let's not take chances. If that scream was made by the demon, he must be in horrific pain." Deacon shut the door before turning out the lights.

They sat on the couch waiting, for what, Lyn wasn't sure. Maybe they waited for a motive to venture into the forest. Perhaps they needed a reason to stay put. When she looked at him, she saw the concern and possible fear in his eyes. The initial fear changed to a surge of adrenalin. "We have to help whoever is out there."

"In the darkness? That would be too dangerous," Deacon said. "We'll wait until first light. Becoming another victim is not something I plan to allow."

"We don't even know if there is a victim," Lyn countered, knowing Deacon was right.

"The scream we just heard was not one of pleasure but one of pure hell." Deacon sat down, pulling her next to him. He held her close.

Comfort from his embrace and the closeness she felt gave her reason to think more clearly. A fine line existed between heroism and blindly running into danger. She could tangle with the best and she'd run blindly into danger once before. Not tonight.

"Waiting until morning," she paused. "Waiting until morning to search out this person or animal might be too late."

"True," he said. "But we have no choice."

"Even with our cat eyes? We can see well in the dark." She wanted to explore every avenue before she gave up.

"It's still dark, nearly black. The moon is small and will give no additional light." Deacon stroked her arm then wrapped his hands around her, pulling her against him.

"I won't be able to sleep."

"I won't either. So let's relax and wait for morning light. It's only a few hours away."

Lyn's cell rang. "It's Brody. Hello. It's on speaker."

"Everything ok your way?" Brody asked.

"Yes, you must have heard it to."

"We did and it took all of my older brother antics to keep Carr and Angel from running into the forest to help the poor creature. Balor seems to bring down the wrath of the gods on his head wherever that demon goes."

"That was Balor? Brody, how do you know?" Lyn felt shockwaves reverberate throughout her body.

"We've heard that scream before. Not so ear-piercing or filled with pain, but I recognized it."

Silence followed. Lyn didn't want to put words to her thoughts but, "Do you think Baylor stepped in a lair."

"The idea crossed my mind. He'll be in untold pain, but there really is nothing we can do about it. Traps are set throughout that forest, and I won't have any of us fall into one, Lyn."

"Her tender heart wants to save the creature who was out to take her life," Deacon said.

"Nothing has changed, Lyn. Either he dies or your life will be forever in jeopardy. I know it goes against all we've been taught, but we have to take his life. The council and our clan have given their approval," Carr spoke, his voice solemn and sounding like the world leader he'd become.

"When they find out it's not a cat, perhaps the poachers will ease his pain and shoot him." Deacon muttered, fidgeting with the magazines in front of him.

"I hope not. From some of the reports I've heard, I think our demon would like to find eternity and a bit of rest. Killing him may be just what he wants."

"Who would want to die?" The adrenalin surge had vanished and now curiosity rushed to the prominent part of Lyn's thoughts.

"I don't know. I can only guess, but perhaps someone who'd known the peace of death," Brody said.

"He has no life here. He doesn't know the language, doesn't know how to do anything in this century. How he managed to drive that jeep is beyond me," Carr said.

"Maybe Balor's death would give him the peace he sought. Perhaps it was for the best." Lyn didn't think so, but she was willing to give Carr's words a chance. It was something she needed to think about.

"We have a few hours before sunrise. Since you two are well and safe, you should get some rest," Brody told them.

"You too. But I think I'll run a bath then go upstairs for breakfast. They will be open soon and I want to get an early start. I want to find Balor before the poachers."

"We'll meet you there in two hours. Bye."

Lyn felt the trembling from head to toe as adrenalin pumped throughout her system. "What do you think of all that?"

"Your brother is right. Balor will be dealt with just as we'd planned. He won't escape his fate."

Lyn leaned against Deacon. Her head ablaze with thoughts and feelings she didn't understand. Lost in a maze might be an appropriate way to define her emotions. She didn't want to kill Balor, but if what they guessed might be true and he really did want to die...

"It's one thing to kill someone in self-defense, but murdering a helpless person is not something I want to be part of."

Deacon ran a finger along her neck, pulling hair from her face before kissing her cheek. "I don't want to be part of it either, but what else can we do?"

"There has got to be another way."

"I'd like to know what that is."

~ * ~

Deacon wasn't quite so tender hearted as Lyn, but killing someone who was helpless was not something he could do. Baylor was far from helpless. He had the third eye that he could kill people with. And even though he might want to return to sleep in eternity, he also might want to have company. Lyn would not go with him.

Back to the question at hand, what choices did they have? Kill him or trust him? As far as he could see, there was no reason for trust.

His gaze shifted to the scene outside. A soft glow warmed the horizon. Lyn had fallen asleep on his chest. He nudged her awake.

"Want me to run your bath for you?" He whispered next to her ear, loving the scent of her hair. If he didn't have to find the demon, he could think of another way he'd like this day to play out.

"Oh, my." She sat up and brushed hair from her face. "Did I fall asleep?" She pushed away from Deacon.

"About thirty minutes. We're due for breakfast in a little while." He touched the bottom of her chin with the tip of his finger, lifting it to brush a soft kiss on her lips.

"Bath? My bath, no, I want a shower. I'll hurry." She jumped from his arms and rushed to the bathroom.

A few minutes later he heard the sound of running water then her off-key singing. He grinned.

They would be going into danger, unknowing what to expect. His heart pounded with fear for Lyn and his gut told him to make her stay at the condo, but he knew she'd refuse. With nothing to do but wait for her he tidied the room. Fidgeting, he paced, walked outside then back.

"I'm ready," From behind Lyn wrapped her arms around him. "Let's get this done."

Enjoying the warmth and the gesture, he turned her so they were facing each other. With smiling eyes, she gazed at him and he fell deeper in love. He held her face between his hands and lowered his mouth to her lips. The kiss was a daytime kiss, filled with promises of what could be if time allowed them to pursue more sensual pleasure. Slowly, he pulled away then brushed her lips with a finger.

"Let's go then."

"Are you hungry?" she asked. "It seems all we've done since we arrived in Greece is eat. I've probably gained five pounds."

"Famished and well...you look as if you've lost weight." Now that he looked at her body, he knew she'd lost some weight. Her face was thinner and her eyes were shadowed. He needed to take better care of his mate.

In front of a mirror, she turned from side to side. "Nope." Then she reached out for him.

Hand in hand they walked up the stairs to the rooftop. A waitress met them near the door and jotted down their room number. Deacon watched as Lyn poured her coffee then wandered through the food displays. He wondered about her choices. The same as yesterday and the day before, or would she try something new?

He rarely varied his breakfast until Greece. They didn't offer cereal and skim milk so he'd been forced to branch out and try something different. Today he was going to have the yogurt with honey, eggs and ham and a couple of pieces of bread. If he was right, they were going to be busy most of the day.

After Lyn circled the food area once, she set her coffee cup on a table looking over the ocean. A few minutes later she returned with her food. Dipping her fork into the plate of eggs, she scooped a mouthful and ate, a pensive look in her eyes.

Chattering tourists surrounded them. Some spoke of the eerie scream from the night before and wondered what could have made such a horrific sound. Some wondered if it had been the person or creatures that had seemed to materialize out of nowhere over Bourtzi Island.

Speculation ran rampant. If Deacon hadn't been so concerned about Balor and what had happened to him, he might have found all of this amusing. But he was worried.

"Hey, see you've eaten already." Brody pulled out a chair and turning it around, he sat down resting his forearms on the back. He was dressed in jeans and a shirt, his cowboy hat he held then placed it on his head.

"We have," Deacon sat back, crossing his arms over his chest, watching Lyn enjoy her coffee. "Better eat. Everyone around here is talking about the scream and I'm afraid a few of the crazier folks might venture into the woods. We need to take care of the situation before anyone is hurt."

Brody nodded, agreeing with Deacon. Carr sat down with a plate piled high and Angel followed.

"Okay, I'll get food," Brody said.

Minutes later the foursome strode into a forest that was strangely quiet. Deacon searched the trails for clues. Footprints in the soft dirt told a story—one he didn't like.

As he'd foreseen, inquisitive tourists and village folk had ventured into the woods to see what had appeared suddenly from the fort on Bourtzi Island. Thinking about Balor and his possible reaction to these people enveloped him in a cold sweat.

In the distance, he heard muttered oaths and chatter. A whimper caught the breeze.

Balor.

"Did you hear that?" Carr picked up his pace.

"Someone is hurt." Lyn shielded her eyes and peered down the trail. "Do you think it's Balor?"

"After the scream last night, that's a good guess." Deacon prayed the demon hadn't been caught in a snare.

Deacon wiped his forehead with the back of his hand and loosened his collar then he put a hand on Lyn's shoulder. "We need to approach cautiously. Don't know what we're going to see when we find him."

"Or what we're going to do," Carr added with a shrug and a glance down the trail.

"Should we wait for Jonathan and his group?" Lyn asked anxiously.

Deacon looked at her, frustrated. They were probably on the way or were the group of people they'd heard chatting. But Deacon didn't really think Jonathan would give his location away. "I'm sure Jonathan will be along shortly."

"You're right." She stared at her brothers and Deacon as if she waited for them to explain what exactly they meant to do. "So...?"

"Follow the trail and the chatter until we're close enough to see what's happening," Deacon said.

"Do we hide or surprise them?" Lyn asked with a bit of a flippant tone.

Brody nodded down the path. "Just pretend to be tourists out for a walk. If we run into anyone we don't know, we can ask questions."

"If we run into the poachers?" Carr asked.

"We proceed with extreme caution and let Deacon do the talking. He's met them and knows what they expect to hear," Brody said.

"Crazy, though it does sound like a plan." Lyn started down the trail.

"Lyn, you need to stay in the middle. Don't want you first or last." Deacon reached out to pull her back but she moved aside.

"I don't need that much protection," she told them as she waited for Deacon to move past her.

Deacon glanced at her apologetically as he started to pass her. He took her hand in his and nodded for her to walk along side. "Sorry, I just don't want anything to happen to you. And in our human forms, your strength doesn't measure up to mine or your brother's. The poachers are ruthless and unpredictable."

"All right then." She squeezed his hand.

With that simple gesture he knew she understood, might not like it, but understood.

"We should call the police," Carr said.

Deacon shrugged. "Can if you want, but my understanding is that they can't or won't take the initiative in this matter. They've been given many opportunities but haven't taken one of them. It doesn't seem as if they care or they don't understand the urgency. Instead, they look the other way."

"Then we'll leave it to our vigilante group if the poachers are out in force?" Lyn questioned.

"Balor is not a tiger. He's safe from the poachers, but not the curious. I'm afraid of what the demon will do if he's cornered." Deacon picked up his pace, giving Lyn a little tug.

Brody frowned. "What can he do? Does he have some supernatural power we're unaware of?"

"You're forgetting his third eye." Lyn quickened her stride. "He can kill people with one look if he wants."

A rustle of leaves behind them sent a jab of adrenalin through his heart. He spun and reflexively pulled Lyn behind him. Deacon got his first good look at the man behind them.

"Jonathan, why am I not surprised?"

Jonathan stepped forward. "I could say the same." His voice held both hope and trepidation. "I feel this is the beginning of the end. One way or the other we're going to finish this today."

"Overconfidence doesn't usually work in your favor," Deacon reminded Jonathan.

'Oh." She stared at Jonathan. "So now what?"

"Always to the point," Deacon said.

"We've got to find Balor," Lyn reminded everyone. "And help him."

He was grateful to Jonathan and his work to end the poachers, but he knew the difficult task wouldn't be easily resolved. The shifters working with him were dedicated, loyal, diligent—and knew their survival was dependent upon fighting the poachers, not just convincing them there were no tigers in Greece but ending their criminal activities. For all of that to happen, law enforcement would have to enter the picture.

A loud cry reverberated through the forest, then accompanied by yelling. Another cry of alarm shook the air.

"He's killing people," Lyn whispered.

"Stay here." Deacon turned to Lyn.

She shook her head. "No. It's my life he wants and I'm going to stop him."

He inhaled a swift deep breath of air. "Ok." He grabbed her hand and running behind her brothers, Angel and Jonathan, they followed. A few minutes later they stumbled upon a group of about thirty people. Some were speaking Greek, some English and a few other languages.

Two lay on the ground, unmoving. A cloud rolled over the sun, darkening the forest. A breeze suddenly stirred the humidity and heat of the day, and Deacon was startled to feel a creeping sensation sweep over him.

He didn't understand the feeling, but he felt sorry for Balor who had one leg caught in a lair and was thrashing wildly around, swinging his arms, his eyes bulging. At the moment his third eye was shut, but Deacon knew he'd used it to keep the crowd from closing on him.

The people had circled him and seemed to be waiting for him to weaken. One man leaned over one of the dead, trying to resuscitate and unmindful of what was now taking place.

"What the hell," Jonathan whispered, "is that?"

"A sea demon," Deacon told him. "He wants Lyn for a sacrifice. Don't look at him. His third eye kills people."

"We're not completely human. Does it have the same affect on shifters?" Jonathan queried.

"Hasn't been tested and I don't want to be the first," Brody said then turned to the circling people. "It's best you all go back to town. We'll take care of this, of him."

"What do you know that we don't?" one man's voice stood out from the ensuing chatter.

"You will have to trust us and forget what you have seen here today. If you don't, more of you will die. I can tell you no more. Take your dead and count your blessing that he did not kill all of you."

Baylor let out a loud roar, putting emphasis on Brody's speech.

Deacon tried to put Lyn behind him, but this time she refused to go. Instead, she stepped forward. "You have no place here and in this time." She spoke to Balor." Your years on earth ended. Life is not for you. You must go back and tell them..."

"Rip," Baylor muttered. "Rip." Then he spoke in Gaelic.

Deacon wasn't sure but he thought Balor agreed with Lyn. He searched his memory for the words, but could find none. Holding out his hands as if he meant no harm, Deacon stepped slowly toward the demon. Balor sat down, looking toward his ankle, tears streaming down his face.

His expression told Deacon more than words could, but freeing Balor from the trap was dangerous—not what he'd intended. Yet killing a helpless creature was not something he felt comfortable with. Killing in battle and in self-defense, yes, but not this.

"What are you doing?" Brody stepped forward, his hand on Deacon's shoulder in an attempt to restrain him.

"I don't know." Deacon pushed hair from his face. "We can't let him suffer. No one deserves this kind of torture."

"We can't free him either." Carr walked to stand next to them.

Instead of dispersing as they were told, the crowd shuffled forward, curious and fearless now that the creature seemed subdued.

Angel turned his attention to the people. "Go, all of you. You have no part in this." His words were uttered with a sharp growl.

The people moved back but seemed reluctant to leave. "What right have you to order us around. You are staying."

"You might be hurt." He pointed to the men carrying the dead. "Do you want to die?"

"No more than you..." the man said.

"We understand this situation. We will take care of Balor."

"You know him?" The crowd sensing this was over and they had seen everything, ventured into the forest and slowly scattered. The man Angel spoke with was the last to leave.

"We will handle this." Angel reiterated then turned back to the dangerous situation.

~ * ~

"RIP!" Baylor cried, lunging at Lyn and flailing his arms. "RIP!" Pain shot through his leg. Excruciating pain. Knowing he deserved this for what he'd conspired didn't help.

The McKennas and Deacon moved back in defense mode, but made no motion to retaliate.

Peace.

Rest.

Kill me.

He tried not to open his third eye, not wanting to kill anyone else. The men who died here had come to torment him further. They shot a dart into his shoulder meant to quiet him. In his mind, they deserved death.

So did he.

Fuck, but he'd spent yesterday wandering the town and the forest searching for food. His stomach had rumbled nonstop. He'd found a tiny spring farther inland where he'd quenched his thirst. Then he'd found hell on earth when his foot set the trap. He'd heard bone crunch.

Now it seemed the McKenna clan weren't going to put an end to his misery. Thoughts swept through his head. Reaching an understanding with these people, urgent. He focused his attention on the man called Deacon, Deacon McClain. He seemed to comprehend his needs.

Formulating the words, he tried to send his thoughts to Deacon, but when the man shook his head, he wanted to weep.

They stood around him, talking and pointing.

Shoot me, please. Shoot me! He yelled but no one seemed to understand. He had to make them see this his way. He opened his third eye, trying not to look at them. All he wanted was to frighten them, scare them into killing him.

"Balor," Lyn spoke. "We can let you live if you promise not to harm me or anyone else."

He thrashed and shook his head. "I don't want to live. Kill me. Death will end my torment." Why did he understand what she said when they couldn't understand him?

"You will have your wish." Deacon said but seemed to back off when he looked at Lyn. "Sorry, she would never forgive me if I killed you."

"You have to kill me." He didn't know what to do or how to convince them. His heart pounded in his throat and with each beat, his leg throbbed.

Angel stared at him. His eye was open but nothing happened.

"I didn't think..." Angel said, "I didn't believe he could kill a shifter with his eye."

"What's it to be," Carr walked to him. "I can heal your leg and you can go in peace with the promise not to harm Lyn or anyone else." Carr looked to Deacon. "Can he understand me?"

"I doubt it," Deacon said.

"Then he has to die." Brody moved forward, gun in hand and leveled at the sea demon.

"No," Lyn whispered. "It's not right."

"We can argue this into eternity, but we all know he's not to be trusted." Brody said.

"Maybe there is another way." Deacon moved toward Baylor and searching for the Gaelic words he'd learned so many years ago. "If you want to die, Baylor, give us a reason to kill you."

"Isn't the fact that he wants to give our sister to the Celtic Sea Monsters for sacrifice enough reason to kill him?" Brody asked.

"No," Lyn said.

Deacon pulled the trap open, releasing the monster. With a roar Balor sprang free, lunging at Lyn, his arms wide.

The shot rang through the forest.

Chapter Nine

"No!" Lyn rushed to Balor's side. Kneeling beside him, her trembling hand on his chest, she knew she would do anything to keep him alive. "Heal him, Carr. Please. We can't let him die like this. It's not fair and it's not right."

"The demon should die. He's a monster and deserves nothing less for killing two of my people." A man stepped from the forest, his words harsh and his expression grim.

"You," Deacon said on a whisper, yet his tone was just as severe. "What are you doing here and what right do you have to pass judgment? This man has done nothing to you."

The poacher lowered his gun and laughed, his demeanor changing in an instant. "He sullied one of our traps. I'm surprised you have so much trouble ending him. We might have caught one of those cats that materialized from the fort, but this fellow took up the space. Besides, he's a disfigured human."

Carr looked at Balor, whose eyes pleaded for something, but it didn't seem they asked for life but death instead. "He doesn't want to live. I cannot heal a man, demon, or otherwise if they don't want life. The feat is not possible."

Lyn's heart went out to the Balor. To Lyn, he no longer seemed like a demon bent on killing her, but a man who deserved better. He'd wanted to live, but must have discovered he wasn't meant to be alive in this century. He'd had his time on earth, and now he was supposed to rest. "He's still suffering, Carr. I can't bear it. You have to help him. His fate can be determined later."

The shot from the poacher's weapon had not killed him. "You need to finish what you began. You need to end his suffering." Brody looked to the gunman.

A demonic grin spread across the poacher's face. He put the gun in the holder. "Why? I don't care what happens to him. One way or the other I'm glad he's out of my snare, but whether he lives or dies means nothing to me. Wouldn't want to be prosecuted for murder."

Lyn understood this man, his unfeeling nature and the cruelty that seemed to simmer deep in his soul. Humanitarianism was not part of his values. "Brody, you have to convince Carr to help him." She tried to stop the blood oozing from his chest, but she had nothing but her hand and the bottom of his shirt to put over the wound. Imploring her brother to understand and help, she turned her attention to him.

Deacon was the first to come to her aid. "This goes against my judgment, but I can't resist those big blue eyes of yours, Sugar. I'm not sure what's going to happen here and I know we could all come to regret this. Balor could still harm you or one of us."

Brody cleared his throat, arms crossed in front of his chest. "What are you going to do when he turns on you? He has the sea creatures to answer to, and if he doesn't deliver, they will put him back in his resting place."

"He's not going to hurt me and I think he wants to be put back in his resting place." Instinct told Lyn that Balor wouldn't harm her. She prayed she wasn't wrong but she couldn't let him suffer, and she wouldn't condone cold-blooded murder. The trap lay on the ground.

Deacon handed the trap to the poacher. "Now go, you've got what you came for."

"Very well," the poacher grabbed the snare before turning to leave. Lyn watched him as well as the other curiosity seekers depart. It seemed she held her breath.

"Now it's your turn, Carr. You have to heal him. The gunshot and the leg wound."

"I hope you know what you're doing." Brody raked his fingers through his hair, the expression on her face clearly told her he didn't like what she'd asked.

"I do," she spoke with assurance then turned to the demon. "You want to live. You know you do."

Balor nodded. Lyn wasn't sure he understood what she'd said.

Carr seemed distraught but he heaved a sigh and crouched beside Balor, his hands hovered over the bullet hole. He closed his eyes while a warm glow spread across Balor.

Balor touched Carr's chest. Lyn saw the ache in his eyes and the desperation. Silently, he pleaded for something.

"This is right." Lyn's confidence superseded her fears. Balor would be an ally. She knew it in her heart. He appeared a lost puppy dog in a world he didn't understand. All he needed was a small bit of kindness.

Balor put his hand on Lyn's, his eyes dripping with tears. "Friend."

"Friends," she told him.

As Carr healed the demon, his breathing grew stronger and his eyes were no longer glazed over.

Lyn had been so focused on Balor and Carr, she hadn't noticed the crowd she'd once thought had dispersed was now back. The rumblings from behind her became menacing. Brody and Deacon worked at pushing them back and keeping them from witnessing what Carr had done, but there was little they could do. Most observed the magic.

When Balor rose, the crowd retreated a few feet, seemingly afraid he'd use his third eye, yet they didn't seem to fear him enough to leave. The man who'd shot Balor stepped forward and pointed his riffle at the demon.

"Put it down." Brody's command echoed through the forest.

"What kind of men are you?" the man asked. "He healed the demon and now you expect me to act as if nothing happened. You're all freaks."

"Nothing happened." Carr stepped forward, his hands fisted. "Your shot was superficial, nothing more."

"I saw you bring that man back from the brink of death."

"Really? I don't understand what you're saying. I did nothing." Carr spread his hands wide.

"But..."

Carr grinned an expression Lyn had seen many times then he shrugged. "Your word against ours. And I don't care who anyone believes. You have no proof anything happened here today."

"I know what I saw."

"Look, why don't all of you go back to town, enjoy your day and don't think about any of this." She wished with all her heart no one had seen what Carr had done. What kind of gossip would be spread throughout?

Balor sat crossed legged, rubbing his head and muttering. When he looked up it seemed Lyn could read his mind.

"No, I don't want you to get rid of them for me. If you killed them all, more questions would be asked, and I don't think any of us want to have to explain ourselves."

Balor nodded his agreement.

With the people dispersed, the McKennas were alone with the demon. Lyn didn't know what to do with him. He was almost seven feet tall. Bringing him back to the condo was not an option, but he needed a sheltered place to sleep and food. Even now she heard the rumblings of his stomach. What had she heard? A way to a man's heart is through his stomach. She wondered if the saying worked for sea demons too. Yet he wasn't really a sea demon, but a man who had cast his fate with the monsters.

"Brody?" She turned to her brother, her mind spinning in circles. "Run into town and buy something for Balor to eat."

"What?" Brody laughed. "Food for the man who wanted to kill you? What will you ask for next? Clothes?"

"Well, he's hungry and I want to find some place for him to sleep. I don't know what's going to happen to him, but we have to think of something. Those men will come back and try to kill him."

"I suppose you're going to bring him home to meet the family too?" Brody's laughter had changed to a menacing tone. "Lyn, a few hours ago his plan was to exchange your life for his. Do you think he's changed?"

"You don't have to tell me twice," she said indignantly. "I think we can find a place for him to live the rest of his days in Cactus Junction. The desert would be perfect. We could make sure he lived in peace."

"Just how do you propose we get him there? We can't put him on an airline," Carr's tone was laced with sarcasm.

Deacon put his hands in the air, shaking his head. "I'm not teleporting that demon. No way..."

"That's brilliant. Of course you are." Lyn smiled. "I'm so glad you volunteered, but first we need to get him food. You know, nourishment. Who's going into town?"

"I will," Deacon muttered. "I need to get away from this circus. Maybe when I get back the four of you will have figured out a way to deal with Balor without bringing him to your home." Deacon spun on a heel and headed toward town.

"Hurry." Lyn called after him, waving at his back.

Lyn smiled. She could hear him muttering until he rounded a bend and was out of sight.

"I don't think you've thought this through." Carr scanned the trail in both directions. "There is no shelter out here, no broken down, abandoned hut. We can't build him a place to stay."

"Of course we can. So, you're willing to help with this too. You could build a lean-to." Lyn put her hands on her hips, studying the terrain.

"We could get him out of here today." Angel spoke up for the first time. "Maybe we can send him back to the Sierra Madres the same way we all came to Nafplio."

"Through the vortex? You think that would work?" Lyn wasn't at all sure about any of this. If it did work, why weren't people disappearing from the fort all of the time?

"That's what I'm talking about. We can swim him over tonight when it's the darkest. No one will see," Brody said. "If Deacon won't teleport him, it's the only way. Besides, we know where we came out; it wasn't exactly inside the fort. It was within a crevice close by."

"If the vortex doesn't work, Deacon won't have a choice." Lyn studied Balor with sadness for the big man. She had a hard time believing he'd meant to send her to her death. He smiled at her before wiping a tear from his face. She nodded and tried to tell him they were going help him and send him to a place where he'd be safe.

"Can he walk?" Carr asked.

She looked at Balor and as if he'd understood Carr's question, he picked up a stick and using it for support, rose.

~ * ~

After rounding a bend in the trail, Deacon set off on an easy run to clear his mind. Lyn's good-hearted feelings could get her into trouble, but he loved her the way she was and would deal with ramifications if necessary. Fuck, he'd even teleport the demon if that was what she wanted, but he hoped they'd find another way.

His smile grew as he approached the town. The incidents that took place this last week had changed and shaped his life in ways he could not have dreamed.

Who would have thought?

Who would have thought?

He certainly had never expected this turn of events--Balor coming to their side and fighting against the poachers, but he still had reservations and he sure as hell meant to keep an eye on that one.

While they'd been in the forest, the sky had clouded over, and now it chose to let loose with a heavy downpour. He covered his head with the hood of his sweatshirt then hoped the clan had found a sheltered spot to put Balor until they could find a way to get him back to the Sierra Madres. Hiding the demon would not be an easy feat. Perhaps he would need to teleport him.

Finally reaching the little town, Deacon took shelter in a small restaurant and sitting near a window to watch the rain, he wrestled with his thoughts. The food he ordered would have to be enough for all of them. He didn't think they'd return to town before they decided how to transport Balor to the cave he'd stumbled upon deep in the Sierra Madres.

He sat down at a table with a small hot coffee he'd ordered while he waited for the to-go meals. Rain sluiced from the sky and rivers swept along the curbed sidewalks. Rain in Greece seldom lasted a long time, but by the look of the dark clouds, he was pretty sure the water wasn't going to let up soon.

The idea of dashing to the condo and retrieving something to ward off the rain flitted in his head, but he thought better of it. Instead, he decided to buy light rain gear for everyone before heading back to meet them.

Fortunately, he was wrong. As quickly as the rain began, it ended. The sun peeked from behind dark clouds that had parted and rays of sunlight warmed the earth. He'd save his shopping expedition for another time.

"Sir," the waiter set the boxes of food on his table. "Your order."

Deacon paid. "Do you have a sack I can use to carry these?"

"I'll get you one." The waiter left and in a few seconds returned to Deacon's table.

"Thanks." Deacon piled the boxes in the sack. For a few moments he stood in the doorway, gazing outside and looking for anyone who might be a threat. He couldn't say he'd made many friends during his stay in Greece. And the few people who he empathized with, couldn't wish him out of their country soon enough.

"Deacon!"

He smiled, knowing that sweet voice anywhere. "Sugar, you came to help?"

"Yup." Lyn slipped her arm into the crook of Deacon's arm. "They were arguing over me and my trust in Balor, so I decided to let them do it alone."

"Glad you came. Do want a coffee before we return to battle your brothers?"

"No, I have to face them sometime, and the sooner I do the better. That comment sounds as if you're on my side now?" She smiled at him, her eyes shining.

He tweaked her on the nose. "I'm on your side, even though I agree with your brothers; Balor could still be a threat to your life."

"Well that's good to know—that you're on my side, not that Balor might want to harm me," she told him, her grin lopsided and sexy as hell. "I don't believe he harbors ill-will when it comes to my life. Now my brothers, on the other hand, might need to watch their backs."

He had a sudden, but not unusual need to make love to her, and he knew the sooner she was his wife, the happier he'd be. "Glad you like my decision. I'll always be on your side even if I might want to talk you out of whatever you're planning." Carnal thoughts not at all appropriate for this moment whirled in his mind.

For a few minutes the pair walked in silence. Natural sounds from the forest echoed around them. But the report of a riffle sent a chill down his spine. Then another followed.

"What was that? A gun shot?" Lyn's fingers tightened around his arm.

"You stay here." He handed over the bag of food.

"Not a chance in hell. If my family is in trouble, I'm going to help."

He turned on her. "You have to stay here. Where it's safe."

She shook her head. "Doesn't matter, you can't make me. I won't take any chances, but I know I can help."

He pulled her close for a quick kiss then took the bag from Lyn. "Let's go then."

More shots reverberated through the trees. Deacon's heart pounded hard as he ran. A quick look over his shoulder told him Lyn kept pace. He tucked the sack under one arm as he ran, and prayed all were safe. Yet the sinking feeling in the pit of his stomach would not go away.

A shot whizzed by his head. He ducked. "Get down," he yelled to Lyn who fell to the earth. "Over here." Deacon crouched behind a large boulder and motioned for Lyn to join him.

"What's happening?"

Whatever it is, it's not good." He stretched to see over the top of the rock. "Fuck!"

"Deacon?"

"Your brothers and Balor have taken refuge behind various trees, and they seem to be trying to lure their attackers into shooting at them, and it looks as if your demon has killed several of the enemy."

"Lyn don't!" His heart pounding, he watched her peer around the corner of the boulder then stand. He reached over to pull her down, but froze when he saw what she was doing.

With a swift sudden sweeping movement of her arm, she sent a current of force toward one of the shooters, the gun flying from his hand. Within seconds, Lyn had disarmed all who posed a threat. He'd never seen anything like it, and had never imagined she had such ability...moving objects without touching them.

She slumped to the ground, her face in her hands. When she looked up, her eyes were dark. "I..."

"Did you know you could do that?" he asked.

She nodded, seemingly speechless for a moment. "I've never done it before—not like that. I've moved little things, mostly to tease my brothers, but nothing of this magnitude."

Her brothers strode toward them.

"That was impressive, little sis." Brody stood beside her a devilish grin on his face.

Deacon lent her a hand, helping her to stand.

"It was?"

Balor hadn't moved. He'd killed seven of the ten poachers. The remaining three had turned and run as soon as they lost their weapons.

Lyn brushed her hands on her pants and leaned into Deacon who pulled her close. "What now? Do you think the poachers will leave? Despite the fact I love this quaint town, I want to see Kimi and spend time on the ranch. I want to go home. I need to feel safe again."

"We go home and leave these people in peace. Don't know what the remaining poachers will do, so hoping they leave is an option," Brody told them.

"I'd like that—the poachers gone, but we won't know for awhile. Actually I'd rather see them all arrested and in jail." Jonathan appeared from the woods, his wife, Cherise, behind him.

"The poachers aren't going to come back. If they do, call us and let us help." Carr extended a hand to shake Jonathan's. "I'm Carr McKenna."

"Well," Jonathan looked around the clearing and down the trail. "We might have solved the problem here, but not around the world. As long as there is such profit in selling everything tiger, there will always be someone to take their place."

Cherise wrapped an arm around her husband. "What are you going to do with him?" She nodded toward the demon.

Brody laughed, a deep belly laugh that Deacon wasn't too sure about. "We are going to take him home with us. Hopefully, the way we came."

Lyn spoke. "He'll have room in the Sierra Madres to live out his life. He can hide in a cave or roam the desert. It will be up to him. Our family will make sure he has everything he needs. He's earned some peace and a life that isn't filled with fear."

"He will be welcome at my home," Deacon couldn't believe what he was saying, but he meant every word.

"Really?" Lyn turned to him. "I never expected..."

"Yes." And he knew from the way her summer blue eyes shimmered with unshed tears, he would always try to make her happy.

Jonathan took Cherise by the hand. "Then we wish you happy and healthy lives."

And Deacon imagined Jonathan saying *I hope you never return here.*

"The same to you, your wife, and your clan." Carr stepped forward, taking charge of the scene. "Please feel free to visit us at Cactus Junction."

"Thank you," Jonathan said.

Deacon watched the pair disappear down the trail toward town then turned to Lyn. "Time to eat." Then retrieving the sack with lunches, he handed them around.

Balor let out a low growl of what sounded to be appreciation as he opened the box and stared inside. He drank from the water bottle Lyn had given him before saying in stilted English, "Never hurt Sugar."

Deacon let out a loud laugh of approval. "I guess he can call you Sugar as long as he understands you're my Sugar."

Lyn swatted at him. "I'm going to have to get used to that awful name, aren't I?"

"You bet." He bit into his burger. Still, he didn't take his main focus from Balor. Despite all that had happened and their promises to the man, he didn't trust him. Trust would take time.

"We have several hours before we can head to the fort. What do you say we try to teach Balor some more words?" Brody said.

Lyn held up her hand. "Hand," she told him and nodded for him to repeat.

With seeming ease, he repeated the word then about one hundred more. When quizzed, he remembered what he'd learned. "Good job," Lyn was proud of his accomplishment.

"It's time," Brody said. "The sun is setting and we really need to get going. We should all go back to the Sierra Madres the same way we came."

"Does that mean I have to teleport again. I think I'd rather fly."

"If you want to spend time on a plane." Deacon shrugged, not wanting to go that way, but if it's what Lyn wanted, he'd go with her.

Lyn let out a long sigh. "Not really. The food is always so horrible."

"Now that you've done it twice, it won't leave you quite so breathless and look at the rewards. You'll be home in a blink and you'll be able to talk to your twin."

"All right, but only after my brothers, Angel and Balor leave. I want to make sure nothing bad happens and if it does, we'll still be here to help them.

"Is there anything at the condo you can't live without?" Deacon hoped the answer was no. He didn't want to risk returning to town and their place.

She thought for a moment. "I want to go back. We bought some souvenirs. I really do want to bring them home with me. Is it going to be a problem to go to the condo?"

"We need keep a low profile. I don't want any trouble." His heart pounded against his ribs. He wanted to tell her everyone would live without the little souvenirs, but he couldn't.

"We need to pay the bill too."

"That's taken care of. I paid for a week when we arrived. I'm sure the hotel will be more than happy to get a few extra dollars." Deacon didn't want to talk to anyone or see anyone for that matter.

"Okay, then we can go back after dark and after we're sure the guys are able to get to the fort and the vortex without being seen. After that, they're on their own."

They walked to a fairly secluded place on the beach and watched as the men waded into the water and swam to the fort. Swimming in just pants, the journey was slow, but when they reached the fort they turned and waved.

A few moments later they disappeared around the structure. "Do you think they'll end up in the cave?"

Deacon didn't know. "I hope so. The odds are stacked in their favor." Minutes ticked by, and there were no fireworks or explosions only silence. Deacon felt Lyn's body shaking and pulled her close. Her warmth next to him gave him peace of mind, and he knew she was his for eternity.

"I'm sure they made it. They should be in the cave as we speak, so it's time for us to do what needs to be done."

~ * ~

Balor knew the McKennas didn't trust him, but they didn't understand how sweet Sugar had stolen his heart. He'd fight all of the demons in hell to keep her safe. There was nothing that would stand between him and her life.

By the time they reached the island, his arms and legs felt like logs. His breaths came in short tight pants. The McKennas had made him swim in front, slowing down each time he did and watching him. He could feel their hot gazes on the back of his head. While he didn't blame them, he hoped some day he could gain their trust.

Once on dry land, he stopped for Carr, Brody, and Angel. He didn't know where they were going, or if there was a plan. The portal they were ejected from hadn't been inside the fort, yet he didn't know how to locate the black hole. Goosebumps slithered down his spine. The unknown terrified him.

Behind him the clan was talking, but he only heard parts of the conversation. Surprisingly, he was picking up more words each time someone spoke. Sugar, he understood better than anyone else. It was something about her eyes that helped him comprehend what she was saying, or maybe what she was thinking.

The oldest, Brody, gestured to him to walk around the corner. Balor followed the oldest sibling, stepping along the rocky path, stones cutting into his feet and his heart pounding in his chest, his wet pants clinging to his legs.

A door in the fort slowly opened. Brody motioned for him to walk inside first. He swallowed hard, easing sideways through the opening and bending over at the waist so as not to hit his head on the top.

"Think Crystal Cave," Carr said. "If all of us focus on that, we can pray that's where we'll end up."

"Pray being the operative word," Angel spoke.

Balor felt them behind him, heard their breaths, felt their apprehension. It was the same for him, fear, apprehension, and terror. There had been so many new experiences in his life; he wasn't open for any more. He took solace in the thought that if he died, he could rest in peace for all of eternity. He never again wanted to be brought back to life.

Once was enough and he'd learned his lesson if there was anything to learn.

Inside, steps wound downward in a spiral fashion. He vaguely remembered crawling on all fours to get out. A few steps and darkness enveloped him. He put out his hands, hoping to feel something with his hands before it hit him.

"You sure this is the hole we were thrown from?" Carr asked.

"Sure as I can be," Brody replied and Angel grunted.

For a moment he thought about looking at them to see if he could read anything from the expression on their faces, but chose not to turn, knowing the blackness of the space wouldn't allow it. Instead, he walked farther down the steps, the air smelling musty, breezy currents swirling around his body.

"Stop," Brody commanded.

He halted on what appeared to be a circular platform, the shifters following suit and joining hands. His pulse thrummed in his head, energy spun and a beam of light encircled the men.

"Crystal Cave, Crystal Cave," they murmured.

His body rose from the floor, and he flew through a tunnel, thrown from side to side as the vortex enveloped all of them. He felt bile burn the back of his throat and forced it down. Wind whistled around his ears, his heart stopping for a moment then speeding once more. Sleep in eternity never seemed better, but these men wanted him alive. For what purpose he didn't know.

The tunnel spit him onto the floor of a dark space, the others tumbling around him.

"Fuck."

"Damn."

"Shit."

The men cursed, their voices bouncing from the walls as they hit the solid rock floor. Silence followed and Balor felt a tiny smile grow. Rubbing his neck with one hand and using the other to help him rise from the floor, he waited for more instructions.

"Guess our thoughts got us to the right place." Brody swept his hair from his eyes. Standing, he surveyed the place they'd landed.

"Yeah, here we are, and what are we going to do with Balor?" Carr asked. "We can't leave him here. He could end up who knows where."

"There are plenty of caves in the area," Brody said.

"You could take him to your great grandfather's home. Balor could help out. Grandfather can always use an extra hand for his ranch."

Balor's hands rose as if he could stop the disapproval that was sure to follow his words.

Angel continued, "Grandfather would understand Balor. And Balor would have a place of safety, food and shelter."

"You're presuming a lot." Carr's voice was harsh with displeasure. "I don't want harm to come to grandfather."

"Hold on a minute. Angel might have a point." Brody looked pensive. "Let's run it by father and see what he has to say about this."

Who the hell is their great grandfather, and why would I stay or go for that matter?

"Why would father say anything?" Carr strode from the cave shaking his head. He turned, "I'm saying, no."

Chapter Ten

"Wow, that wasn't half as bad as the first time." Lyn turned to face Deacon and placing her hands on both sides of his face, she pulled him to her for a kiss.

In his arms, he shifted her to accommodate the kiss. His tongue delved into her mouth, playing with her. She loved his kisses, never wanted them to end, but she knew this one had to come to a halt. Before he could stop it, she moved her hand to run her fingers through his hair, heard his groan of pleasure.

With a smile, she moved back. "I love you, Deacon."

"Ah, Sugar, I love you more. Is there a private place anywhere close?" His eyebrows lifted, suggesting sex was on his mind.

Lyn wriggled free to set her feet on the ground. "Hold that thought. We have to go home and see what happened to Balor, my brothers and my cousin. I'm dying to see if Balor is still alive."

"Your brothers will honor your wishes." Deacon ruffled her hair. "They will not harm him."

"I know..." Deep down she understood they would not kill Balor, but there was also an underlying fear that harm would find its way to him. His innocence in a time well beyond his understanding could be his undoing.

"How far to the ranch? I'm dying to meet your mom and dad." Deacon took her hand in his, waiting for direction.

"You did okay on the landing. Our house is about ten miles south. You ended up closer to Crystal Cave than the ranch." She tugged on him. "I want to see Kimi. Let's get going. I'll race you to the horses."

"What's all that noise?" Deacon's brows furrowed.

"Sounds like a war." Their walk changed to a run and as they crested a hill near the cave Lyn heard the roar of a Jaguar and recognized Carr, then Brody and the growl of a lone wolf. She listened for Kimi, but didn't hear her. Relief swept through her. Kimi didn't belong in a fight. Then adrenalin rushed within and the thrill of the coming events.

Deacon tugged on her hand, stopping her. He bent down and gave her a quick kiss, "Be careful."

They ran until they saw dust flying and sparks filling the air. This was not a fight against Balor. The demon was in the middle of a large circle of green-slimed men she didn't recognize.

And Kimi...

Kimi's hands were in the air and bolts of electricity shot from them. Her aim was lacking. She missed her mark more than she hit.

I guess you found your second gift, little sis.

"Stay here," Deacon held out his arm.

Indignation coursed through her. "You can't be serious. Why?" She held her breath after asking the question. The answer was clear. If the demons saw her, they would have the upper hand if they could grab her.

"You know why."

"Then you shouldn't go down there either. They seem to have everything under control, and I'm sure I need protection."

Deacon let out a bellow of laughter. "Crazy girl. Are you trying to provoke me? It's not working, but I am going to stay here unless the crew below needs help then we'll both go to work."

"Okay, we'll sit back and watch the fireworks. Look," she pointed to the field where the battle was taking place, "Kimi hit one. Kimi...behind you."

Lyn stood and swept her hand across her body, her gaze focused on one of the sea demons. He flew through the air, landing almost one hundred feet from Kimi. Whirling, Kimi looked at her sister, but that gesture turned everyone else's focus to the hill.

"Damn," Deacon swore. "They're all headed this way." Before Lyn reacted to his comment, he'd shifted. A deep breath of air later she stood with her feet firm on the ground and used her powers to throw the demons through the air.

When Balor saw the sea creatures head toward her, he let out a bellow of rage. Kimi saw too and this time her flames hit the target and one went down. Carr, Brody, and Angel had shifted earlier.

Carr swiped his claws across the face of his enemy then crushed his jugular. Brody had killed his victim moments after and when he lifted his face from the enemy's' neck, he let out a roar. Angel chased one then leaping on the demons back, they pummeled to the earth. His kill wasn't as easy. The demon rose from the earth and threw Angel off his back.

Stronger and quicker than the demon, Angel attacked. The fight lasted seconds before the demon met his maker.

Now there were three left. They raced up the hill, chasing the demons. Deacon stood in front of Lyn and with a low growl, waited. Lyn stepped to Deacon's side before she waved her hand in the air once more and one demon flew back to meet his end at the hands of Brody. Kimi sent a bolt of lightning through another and that left one.

Deacon charged down the hill and in one powerful leap sent the enemy sprawling to the earth. A second later the last foe was dead.

Lyn let her hands fall to her sides, closing her eyes and inhaling deep life giving air. Deacon didn't shift back but stood next to her, touching her as if he needed to make sure she lived. She rested her hand on his head. The security he gave her overwhelmed and filled her with a sense of coming home.

Kimi walked toward her, her hands out stretched. They embraced.

"You do have a second power," Kimi beamed, so proud of her big sis.

"I do and I think it's going to come in handy. It's nice to be able to fight without baring my claws. I had no idea it was so powerful until we were in Greece."

"Yeah, in this family it appears we need all and any weapons," Kimi said. "I just discovered my power today."

"Were those the sea demons who sent Balor to kill me?"

"The green slime gave it away?" Kimi laughed. "When they went after Balor, the clan gathered together and stood beside him. We had to after he fought for you and Deacon."

"I wasn't sure, but I guessed. They had a distinct fishy odor too. Glad we arrived in time to help. My prayer is to never, ever see another demon of any kind."

Lyn watched the brothers and cousin lope toward Crystal Cave. "They have clothes stashed nearby?"

"Nope."

"I don't get it." Lyn watched the trio disappear in the hole on the side of the hill.

"That they don't have clothes?"

"That you're here. How did you know to come?" Lyn frowned, searching Kimi's face.

"Coincidence." She shrugged. "Dad wanted me to check on you guys. Didn't know if you'd come to the ranch or the cave. Kinda figured you'd arrive at the cave."

"Deacon." Lyn knelt beside him. "Go with my brothers. We'll bring clothes." When he looked hesitant, "Go on. I'll be fine. I have my fire-shooting sister to protect me."

The big cat shook his head, but followed the McKenna brothers.

Kimi chuckled. "Doesn't want to leave you, does he?"

"He has this protective instinct. I can say without hesitation that I love knowing he wants to shield me from harm. Sometime he goes a bit overboard. His instincts kick in and he loses control."

"Doesn't he know you can take care of yourself?" Kimi frowned, her eyes narrowing as if concentrating. "That's like Mak."

"Okay, hold up. First question, he knows I can but he still wants to protect me and who is Mak?"

"A friend of Angel's." Kimi's cheeks turned a sweet shade of pink and she danced a bit away from her big sis.

"Fess up. Is he your mate?" It seemed while she'd been away, Kimi had gone on with her life.

"Don't know. He doesn't talk to me much, just looks my way when he thinks I won't see, but I get this feeling every time we get close. Is Deacon your mate?"

Lyn inhaled a deep breath. "That's right, you don't know. A lot has happened in this last week. A lot." They linked arms and walked down the hill. "The horses close by?" Lyn wanted to tell Kimi everything, but not until they could sit down with a glass of wine, not until they could be just sisters.

"Yup and I have enough for all of us. Dad thought of everything. He drove up here with me so we took two trailers." Letting go of Lyn, Kimi skipped down the hill. "It's going to take some time. Hope the guys will be all right. And don't think for one moment that I forgot what I asked you."

"Of course we will," Lyn paused. "I want to tell you about Deacon and me, but I want the time and the privacy. Ok?"

"I'm holding you to that."

"And I'll get to meet Mak?" They reached the horses. It would take a better part of the day to ride to the truck and horse trailers. Tomorrow would be here before they returned.

Lyn was tired, exhausted. Hurtling through time took every ounce of energy from her. All she wanted at the moment was to snuggle next to Deacon in a soft bed and sleep for twenty-four hours. Instead, she looked at long hours of riding then driving before she could have the privacy she desired. Never mind the sleeping and snuggling.

Mid-afternoon, the pair reached the truck. The journey had been uneventful, no more sea creatures attacking. Hot and sweaty, Lyn wanted a shower and a good night's sleep, but she imagined the men, waiting in the dark for their clothes. By the time they finally returned, they would be irritable and ready for action.

"What was Greece like?" Kimi swung from the saddle. It was her first question since they started the ride.

"Beautiful, want to go there?" The trip had been wonderful in many ways. She'd met her mate, made love and fallen in love. Even though she'd become a homebody at heart, she wanted to go back. At times when they were not hiding from poachers, the life there was idyllic, time seemed to go by at a slower pace.

"I would like to travel everywhere in the world. I want to see Athens, Rome, Paris, and more. Everything," Kimi said.

They led their horses into the trailer. "That's quite the agenda, Kimi, everywhere?"

"Is there something wrong with that?" Kimi sounded indignant.

"Now don't get all defensive on me. Of course there's nothing wrong. Let's get these horses back to the ranch so we can rescue our men."

~ * ~

The breathtaking early morning sunrise put a smile in Lyn's heart and soul. They had arrived at the ranch in time for dinner and a quick nap before starting back to the cave. Finding clothing large enough for Balor had been a challenge, but in the end, they discovered some larger pants and shirts in the attic left behind by a former ranch hand.

Sean, Deacon's father, made the trip to Crystal Cave with her. She had mixed feelings. Needing privacy was important to her, but after yesterday's events, she knew protection was the only option.

"You and Deke figure out what you have together?" Sean rubbed his chin before slanting her a challenging grin. "I'm hopin' to see a few grandkids running around pretty soon."

Lyn felt the blush from her forehead to the tips of her toes. She cleared her throat bent on telling this man, who she barely knew, as little as possible. "We are, as you say, figuring it out." Staying calm and enduring this discussion was easier said than done.

He let out a short belt of laughter. "I bet you are. I didn't embarrass you did I? Sorry."

"What does that mean? And no, you didn't embarrass me, so you don't need to apologize." The tone of his voice set her on edge and more defensive than she'd ever felt in her life. "Maybe you should ask your son."

"I will..." He laughed again then started humming.

"I bet you will." Lyn wasn't sure why she'd turned surly. But her thoughts were so new and so private. The last thing she wanted to do was share.

From that point they rode in silence until the opening of cave grew large enough to see from the trail. Her thoughts went to Deacon, inside the cave, naked. She swallowed hard, hoping Sean couldn't read her mind.

"Is that it up yonder?" Sean pointed a finger in the general direction of the cave.

Lyn wondered why Deacon didn't have the old west twang in his speech like his father then filed it away for a future question when they were alone. "Yes."

Sean kicked his horse into a trot, seeming eager to see his son. Lyn didn't like playing seconds, but Deacon had put his life on the line for hers and she supposed a father would want to see his son. She reigned in and shielded her eyes, hoping for the needed patience.

Minutes later they were at the entrance. "You in there, Deke?" He dismounted the horse in moments, and grabbing the saddlebag, sauntered into the cave.

Lyn waited for the men to emerge. Seconds changed to minutes and finally Deacon and the rest strode from the dark mouth. Lyn's heart skipped a beat, then without more thought, she raced to him and flung her arms around her man. He picked her up and spun her around her feet in the air.

While Deacon twirled her in circles, she whispered, "I missed you."

"Me too," he told her back. "I'll save that thought for when we're alone." He gave her a quick kiss before setting her down.

"Promise?" Her feet touched the ground.

"Yeah, I promise." He took her hand in his as they walked to the horses for the ride home.

Chatter behind Lyn was hard to hear. Her concentration was focused on Deacon, but she couldn't help pick out a few phrases. She heard Balor's name more than anything else.

Then no one walked behind them, heated voices filled the air. Her heart in her throat, she turned, motioning for Deacon to follow. The gist of what her brothers were saying did not sit right with her.

"What are all of you discussing? Or should I say arguing about?" Even though she asked, she was sure she knew the answer, but she wanted someone to acknowledge it.

"We're trying to decide what to do with the demon." Brody ran his fingers through his hair as his brows furrowed. "You know we don't trust him, can't trust him, won't ever trust him."

"I thought we decided to take him to great grandfather's ranch." Lyn understood that was the only place he could survive. He couldn't live on his own. He didn't have the resources but he could live and help with chores on the spread in exchange for food and clothing. Great grandfather would love him and respect him for who he was.

"Well," Carr was hesitant. "We're still not sure where his loyalties lie. I'm with Brody on the matter of trust. He could turn on any of us and then..." Carr shrugged.

"He didn't prove himself in the last battle? He didn't put his life on the line for the McKennas—twice?" With a frustration coupled with anger, Lyn rarely felt around her brothers she shook one finger at them. "He did more than that. I can't believe those words, Carr McKenna. He fought two battles in my defense. He's earned the right to some peace and quiet in his life."

Carr stepped back, holding his hands in front of him. "You can't blame a soul for their suspicions. I want to make sure you're safe."

"You're thoughts and fears are groundless. Who's going to take him up the mountain to the ranch? If no one volunteers, Deacon and I will be pleased to do the duty."

"No, you need to see the clan and tell your story, maybe have some debriefing. Carr and I will take him, but I don't know how to tell him. All he's done is sit in the corner of the cave, moping."

"I'll tell him."

Lyn walked to Balor and took his hand in hers then looking into his eyes, she spoke slowly. "Balor, we talked about this, and I believe the safest and most comfortable place for you is up the mountain."

Balor looked where Lyn had pointed then nodded with a slight grunt of what sounded as agreement.

Lyn went on, "Carr and Brody are going to show you the way to our great grandfather's ranch. You can work at whatever you do best for food and clothing."

Again, Balor nodded then said, "Okay."

"I'll go with your brothers if that's all right," Sean said.

She smiled. "Well then, okay. Carr, Brody, get your horses and help Balor." She walked back to Balor. "Can you ride a horse?"

He grinned and smiled. "Yes." His speech was hesitant.

Amazed Lyn now knew Balor would make it. He was a fast learner, picking up language quickly. She found herself growing rather fond of the giant, a man whose decision-making was flawed.

The man stood and Lyn gave him a big hug before letting him go. She watched with a hopeful heart as Balor strode through the opening of the cave with her brothers behind him.

Then he turned, "Will I see you again?"

Tears formed in Lyn's eyes and she wiped them away with the back of her hand. "You will. In a week or so."

"One week," he parroted. "Promise?"

"Promise."

Lyn hoped he understood what she'd tried to say, hoped he wouldn't be afraid, but she knew he was strong and resilient. Knew her great grandfather would take good care of him, teach him things he would need to learn.

~ * ~

"Come on, Sugar, Balor is going to be just fine." Deacon wanted to reassure Lyn, understood her need to go with the big guy and respected her decision to return to the McKenna ranch.

"I wish I could be two places at the same time." Then she held her hands in front of her. "No, I don't want to teleport, and that's not the same."

"I wouldn't think of it. One can only fly through space on occasion. The sensations are too intense to make a habit of it." Deacon wrapped his arm around her shoulder. "How long will the ride back take?"

"We can make it to the truck and trailer by nightfall, then home or we can stay a night in the desert."

He thought about her invitation. When they arrived at the ranch, they wouldn't have a moment's peace, and they wouldn't be allowed to sleep together. He felt a strong need to be alone with her, to show her once more how he felt about her. And, he wanted to ask her to marry him. If he didn't do it tonight, the words might be put on hold for a few more days and he didn't want to wait.

"We're going to spend the night. We have some unfinished business." He felt his grin spread across his face.

She stared at him, a quizzical expression on her face then she cocked her head to one side. "What unfinished business?"

He grinned and tweaked her nose. "It's a surprise." They reached the horses.

"Did I tell you, I don't like surprises?" She patted her horse's nose before she mounted, waiting for his response.

He smiled, following her lead, mounting his horse. "I learn something knew about you everyday."

"Tell me."

"Nope, when the time is right, you'll know what unfinished business I'm speaking of." If he was honest with himself, he would have liked to sweep her off her horse and ask her right now, but she deserved romance.

He felt the silent daggers stabbing him in the back as they rode down the trail, and he almost caved. But, damn it, this was important. The proposal had to be done right or he'd hate himself for the rest of his life. Now, he wasn't a romantic, but he knew she was.

"I don't like to wait." She rode beside him. "Tell me, please. Pretty please with sugar on top."

"You're playing dirty." That please tugged at his heartstrings. He dug down deep to find some resolve and pulled it to the forefront of his mind. "No, I can't."

"You won't."

"Right. I won't and I can't. I want everything to be perfect." If she kept this up, she'd guess what he had in mind and he didn't want that either. "What's your favorite food?" A change of subject could always come in handy.

"I know what you're up to, buddy."

"And what is that?" So far so good, subject changed.

"You're changing the subject."

"Is it working?"

"Yes," she gave a huge sigh. "I guess I need to grow up. I can wait for you to spring something on me. But you could give me a hint."

"And play twenty questions? Nope."

"I get it. You're not a pushover."

"I'm not and you won't be disappointed. Now, I really do want to know what your favorite food is."

"Guess."

"Aw...retaliation. You're going to make me work for this one."

"Yes. Guess you have to play anyway."

"Okay, let me think. You really liked the chicken souvlaki we had in Nafplio."

"Nope. I mean, I liked it, but it's not my favorite."

"A Greek salad?"

"Close second." She clearly enjoyed his squirming.

"Pizza?"

She laughed and it warmed his heart that she was enjoying herself.

"Nope."

"Can you give me a hint? Will we have a tent tonight? You thought to put a tent in the trailer and food?"

"Yes to the tent. It was father's idea, strange as that sounds and maybe the food I brought is my favorite."

"So we'll both find out tonight—my surprise—your favorite food."

"Maybe I said, and maybe you should keep guessing." At least time was passing quickly. The sooner they settled themselves she would find out.

"I'd rather wait."

"You're no fun. What's your favorite food?"

"Steak." There was no hesitation. "I love my meat. Chicken is okay but I'd rather have a good cut of beef."

They rode in silence for a few minutes. "I don't really have a favorite food. I like everything, hence my eating disorder."

"I forgot about that. You seem so normal now."

"Yeah, but I've had years of counseling. I've never been overweight. I don't know where or how it came about, but, hey, we've better things to talk about. I think I'm cured now."

"You seem to be all right. I'd notice if you didn't eat." Concern for her swamped him. He didn't know how to deal with eating problems.

"I am. I'm fine. Look at that sunset." She pointed to the west. "The colors seem to blend together."

"It's awesome." He wanted to pull her into his arms and kiss her. "How much farther?" He readjusted himself in his saddle, suddenly feeling a bit uncomfortable.

"Over that hill. We can brush the horses down, set up the tent then eat." Maybe they'd make love first.

~ * ~

Balor liked the great grandfather. When Lyn had told him he was going into the hills, he'd thought at first they were abandoning him. But the elder had taken to him, giving him a huge hug and grin.

"Welcome, Balor of the Celts."

"Thank you."

Balor couldn't help the smile in his heart. The countryside was the exact opposite to Ireland. Barren and harsh, sagebrush littered the land instead of the emerald green of the Isles, yet still he loved the landscape. He could be happy here if given the chance.

"Come, are you hungry?" Great Grandfather linked his arm with Balor's. "Steak and potatoes and a few green beans should put some meat back on your bones. I heard you weren't living too well."

"Hungry." Balor nodded toward the kitchen. "Eat lots." As if to answer, his stomach rumbled.

Great Grandfather laughed. "My cook's the very best. She appreciates a man with a hearty appetite."

After the meal, Balor explored, discovering the outdoor shower. Most of the time in the Isles he would have been cold and wet, but here it seemed most of the weather was hot, sometimes blistering hot.

A screech of a large cat floated on the breeze and Balor was reminded of the McKenna clan and Lyn. He'd fallen half in love with the girl. She was so sweet and beautiful. Damn she was lovely.

Ah, but in another time and place she might have been his. *You're a damn fool, old man.*

A damn fool.

With three eyes, none of the lasses ever took a second look at you, save the ones who wanted your money.

What are they doing, Lyn and Deacon? If she were his lady, they wouldn't go home tonight. No, he'd make love to her in the desert under the light of the rising moon.

Another eerie cry cut through the air, piercing his thoughts.

Chapter Eleven

Lyn stood beside the fire, rubbing her hands on her legs. "Gets cold pretty fast up here. Want to go for a run before we turn in for the night?" Running relaxed her and for some reason her body was so tense she thought it might snap.

Deacon hesitated for a moment, staring at the tent then back to her, "Whatever you want."

"You're acting strange, you know. If you don't want to go, you don't have to, but I need to run."

"If you knew what was on my mind, you'd understand. There's no way in hell I'm going to let you go by yourself."

"Tell me what you're thinking." Lyn leaned into her mate, her lover, and she hoped soon; her husband. Tipping her head to look into his eyes, she moistened her lips in anticipation of the forthcoming kiss.

Deacon grinned, bending toward her. His kiss was sweet and tender, his tongue tracing the seam of her lips. She opened for him, having second thoughts about the run. Maybe sex would relax her and ease the tension.

She sighed and let her tongue meet his, dance, explore. It seemed she also learned something new about him every time she was with him. Her respect for this wonderful man was boundless.

She heard his groan and loved the sound, but weighing her options, she moved away from him.

"If we're going for that run, we better stop this. We can make love after the run." He ran his hands through her hair, looking into her eyes.

"You want me that much?" She knew the answer but she needed to hear him tell her. If she were truthful, she wouldn't mind ripping his clothing off and pulling him inside the tent.

"Of course I do, Sugar, every minute of every day." He ruffled his hair. "Clothes off and you'd better go inside the tent, or I won't take responsibility for my actions."

Lyn pulled him toward her and gave him a quick kiss on the lips. "See you in a few seconds."

Lyn left his side with slow steps. After that kiss, she had third thoughts about the run, but they'd return and take up where they'd left off. The exercise would calm her ragged nerves that were so on edge she couldn't think straight. Not knowing why she was shaky, she needed answers that she believed only he could give her.

With a deep breath, she disrobed then shifted. When she stepped outside, she saw Deacon, his size and strength stole her breath. He was beautiful. Striding to her side, she nuzzled his nose with hers. He purred close to her ear, sending shivers down her spine.

He looked to the west where the sun had nearly set. She nodded and set off in an easy lope before exploding for a few seconds with the speed that was so much a part of her cat world.

Deacon followed her, not attempting to overtake her, which she knew he could. When she slowed, he slowed, when she walked, he followed suit. This pattern continued for about thirty minutes before Lyn changed direction. She stopped, sitting on her haunches and let out a loud screech. Once again, Deacon did the same.

To Lyn, the sound was music, but she understood that with humans the cat screeches could send terror into their hearts.

They walked the remaining mile to the camp, side by side. The camaraderie felt easy and so right. Lyn knew that as soon as they shifted back to human form, they'd make love. Sex with Deacon was incredible. Just thinking about it made her heart race and her body melt. She inhaled a long deep breath, closing her eyes for a quick moment, letting tantalizing thoughts spin throughout her.

Inside the tent, they shifted. Naked, he was gorgeous. He reached out and touched her nipple. The look in his eyes told her he thought she was beautiful. He didn't need words; his expression saying it all.

Then he took her hand in his and led her to the sleeping bags they'd zipped together. Words didn't seem to be needed. She swallowed, her body trembling with need for his touch.

He pulled her close, the feel of his hard body next to hers sent sensations ripping within. She was wet with need and ready for the next step.

"I love you, Sugar."

She wound her fingers in his hair and pulled his head toward her. Their lips met, the kiss mercuric. Without letting go, he swept her into his arms and carried her to their beds.

"I love you too, Deacon, but right now I need you more. Make love to me." She let her head fall back, loving the sensation of his kisses along her neck.

"Me too, and you taste so damn good, Sugar. Open for me. I've needed to do this since I saw you standing outside that damn cave waiting for me."

With a hint of pressure against her back, she moved closer. She felt his cock, hard, hot and ready for her.

Lyn didn't say anything but her mouth opened. His taste was heady as he explored inside her mouth. Teeth, tongue, lips; everything she tasted left her breathless with longing. Holding on to this moment paramount in her head, she met his tongue with hers, danced and played until she heard a masculine groan of pleasure. Every feminine part of her wanted him to set her down on the sleeping bags, but she didn't want him to let go of her.

He let her down easy, but she twisted, wanting to be on top and in control. She straddled him, her legs pressing against his and her hands on his tight abs. Stroking him, she let her fingers trail lower to touch his pulsing cock.

Lyn became the aggressor, the leader in the sexual game they played. Leaning over him, she let her breasts touch his chest, exhilarating in the sensation of her nipples brushing across him. Mouths touching once more, she ran her tongue across his teeth then into his mouth. She moaned with the pure sensations coursing through her. And like an inferno, she thought she might explode from the intense pleasure. Slowly, she pulled back from him, her hands on his biceps.

Inside, her body tightened, clenching with anticipation. She bent over, licking, kissing then gently biting both of his nipples, then trailing kisses downward until she took him inside her mouth. She ran her tongue around the tip then sucked.

His hips bucked then he flipped her over. For a moment she rested, eyes closed, absorbing his heat into her and listening to the pounding of his heart, nirvana to her soul.

She felt kisses across her shoulder, butterfly soft, tender but intoxicating too. Running her fingers through his hair was her silent way of applauding his attentions and asking for more. One of his fingers traced her nipple then squeezed, tugging gently. She couldn't keep a tiny moan of desire from slipping through her lips. Lord, this was sweet, so damn sweet she wanted it to go on forever.

With his mouth, he traced his way up her neck and to her ear, alternating nips and kisses. Against her skin his tongue felt raspy, rough, and it tantalized, heating her body to a mercuric point.

She opened her eyes to look into his beautiful blues.

"Sweet, sweet Sugar," he whispered in her ear. Then his tongue whirled inside, delightfully tracing the lobe. "You are mine, sweetheart, all mine. I will never let you go."

She jumped in his arms. Her fingers roughed through his soft hair then down his back to his muscled tight butt before pulling him closer, reveling in the feel his hard cock nestled against her belly. He was hers and would always be by her side.

He spread her legs and settled between them. Kissing his way from her ear to her mouth then down her neck, he settled against her, the soft buds at the tips of her breasts touching his chest. With teeth, lips, and tongue he paid homage to each one. Her body ignited and she arched her back as if she could summon more from him. He bit and kissed her, then ran his tongue around her nipple.

One hand slid down her stomach to settle on her clit. He worked his magic, touching her as her wall clenched and tightened, then wept for more.

"You are wet for me. I want to taste your cream. But not yet." He kissed her tenderly.

"Deacon," was all she could say.

"I like the sound of my name on your lips." He continued, gently biting then sucking a nipple deep into his mouth, one finger still massaging her clit then moving inside.

An inferno roared to life inside. Suddenly she bucked and moaned, the climax building as he pulled back gazing into her eyes.

"Please," she cried out.

"Keep those baby blues open, Sugar. I want to watch you."

She slid over the precipice, sensation exploding within. She moved with the rhythm he set, one as old as the mountains and as primal as time. When her body stopped bucking and shuddering, he looked at her with an all-knowing grin. "Sugar, you are the most beautiful woman I've ever seen. The sheen on your body makes me want to lick you from head to toe."

"Oh, be still my racing heart." She could barely breathe let alone speak.

He set the palm of his hand above her heart. "I hear the beat. Know that I've surrendered my heart to you."

~ * ~

"I want you again now, and all night long," she told him, her breath a sexy purr as she ran her hands across his torso.

"That's music to my ears." He had to take his time. *Where to start... hmm...* He placed a soft kiss behind her ear. He didn't want to ever stop touching her, holding her. He would never let her go for all of eternity.

"Me too," she told him, her breath a puffy little sigh. She moved against him, tantalizing him and triggering every primal urge he possessed.

"I'm glad. "He purred while his hands roamed the length of her, finding silken flesh he knew he'd never grow tired of possessing. His fingers settled on her belly as his tongue trailed a path across her shoulders. "You taste so good—hot and sweet, a bit salty too."

Her head fell back, giving him more opportunities for exploration. He could see her nipples harden and delighted in the thought he could do that to her. Touching the tip of each one then tracing the aureole, he smiled and murmured. "So damn hot."

She squirmed as if trying to move closer. "Please," she said.

"Damn, Sugar, you don't have to beg. You know you're going to be hotter before we're finished." He kissed across her shoulder while his fingers found each breast and gently squeezed.

"Promise?"

He didn't answer; instead Deacon turned and pulled her on top of him. She straddled him, her core open to his questing fingers. But it wasn't his fingers he wanted inside her. It was his tongue. He needed to taste all of her, every portion he could find. His desire so overwhelming, he didn't want to hold back.

The curls at the apex of her thighs were creamy and white. She was wet for him, needing him, ready for sex. Fascination with her and with her body left him sweating with sexual hunger. She was his, all his. He would never get enough of her.

"I like you naked. I think that whenever we're together you should wear nothing, nothing at all," he murmured as his tongue found a nipple and he sucked it into his mouth.

"Agreed if the gesture is reciprocated. I like you naked too."

Her hands settled on his belly such a short distance from his pulsing cock. But if he let her touch him...

If he let her touch him now, he'd climax without her.

Once again, it seemed to Deacon she meant to take control and he wanted to tell her she could control him any damn time she wanted. She took his nipple into her mouth then bit and laved and teased until he groaned with pure sexual delight.

"Oh, Sugar... It's so, so beautiful, just like you."

Suddenly, he reversed their positions. Now she lay beneath him, her legs spread wide, her long blond hair in gorgeous disarray around her head. He ran his fingers through it, reveling in the soft texture, memorizing the site before tracing her lips with his thumb.

A moment later he kissed his way down her body to her clit. He laved her with his tongue, enticed, caressed and teased. Then his tongue slipped inside her core, felt the walls clench as he sucked and nibbled at the apex of her heated sex. Laving the cream.

Her fingers delved into his hair, and with each movement of his tongue, she bucked against him, pulling on his hair. Her cream tasted so damn sweet. He saw the sheen of sweat glistening on her ivory flesh. She moaned and climaxed, shuddering, and he needed to send her to that heaven once more.

Two climaxes ripped through her body before he kissed his way up her belly, to her breasts, then her lips. She purred softly in the back of her throat, slowly opening her mouth to him. They explored each other with their tongues while his fingers drove inside her tight sheath, sending her to a third pinnacle.

Then he was inside her, matching her pace, and feeling her walls clench his cock. Moments later they climaxed together. For a second he lay on top of her then rolled off, bringing her into his arms, and running his hand down the length of her back.

Taking his time, he brought her down, calming her, soothing her until her heartbeat as well as her breath slowed to a steady even cadence.

"I can't move," she said.

He smoothed her hair away from her face and then kissed each eyebrow. "That's why I'm going to let you rest. Stay here."

Naked, Deacon rose and walked to his satchel near the opening of their tent. He rummaged through his belongings until he found the small box he'd had his father bring from home. When he strode back to the sleeping bags, he watched the play of firelight across Lyn shoulders and face, her body shimmered golden with the colors of warmth.

"God, you're beautiful."

"You are too," she grinned, her focus on him. "What is that?" She pointed to the box.

On one knee he brought her hand to his lips and kissed the back before opening the lid. "Will you marry me? Be my wife? My best friend and confidant?" He took the ring from its resting place and waited.

Her eyes had grown large and the smile beaming from her beautiful lips gave him a small measure of confidence. He watched as she moistened her lips, moisture sparkling in her eyes.

"Yes," she whispered as she watched him slip the engagement ring on her finger. "Yes," she said again.

Seconds later, she was in his arms.

Epilogue

Arm in arm, Deacon and Lyn walked into her parent's ranch house in Cactus Junction. The meeting room had been set up for debriefing. Sean, Deacon's father, sat in a leather armchair in a corner of the room. The McKenna clan was spread throughout. Angel and Phaedra were present as was Mak, who sat next to Kimi.

Lyn's mom walked in with a pitcher of lemonade and a tray of cookies. "I'll bet you two are hungry." She slanted them both a motherly smile which was a bit too all knowing for Lyn and embarrassing as well.

Deacon walked to the matriarch of the clan and standing in front of him, "I would like your permission to marry your daughter, Lyn."

Lyn's Dad beamed then nodded his head as if considering the request. A long pause followed which left Lyn on edge. Then, "I've been wondering if she was your true mate. And you know she is?"

"Yes," Lyn said. *Of course he is*, "I do love him." Her heart leapt and she wiped her sweaty palms on her pants.

Her breath shallow, she waited for the answer. "Of course you have my permission, even though I understand that even if I didn't give it, the two of you would marry."

Heat rose to Lyn's cheeks just as the female part of the clan gathered around her, chatting happily. She understood the relief she felt when her father gave his consent and didn't know what they would have done if he'd refused, even though her father seemed to know.

"When? Have you decided on a date?"

"We're going to have to go into LA to find a dress. I hope we have time."

"A cake."

"Flowers."

"Venue?"

"Music..."

"Hold on. Not so fast. We don't have a date but I want something simple, and I would like to wear mother's wedding dress." She turned to her mom. "Is that all right?" She held her breath waiting for the answer. "Mom?" she queried when too much silence followed her question.

"Of course, sweetheart." She opened her arms and hugged Lyn. "I love you so much, and I'd be so honored if you wore my gown."

"Good, then I'd like the ceremony to take place at the top of Infinity Cliff. I'm hoping that Great Grandfather will marry us in the ways of the Apacheria and that Deacon's father will do the more traditional ceremony." Lyn was pleased with her idea and even more so when Deacon liked it too.

"Beautiful," Kimi sighed. "So romantic."

"We can have cupcakes made at the bakery in town. The music will be a blend of the Native American and Celtic. Deacon, does that work for you?" She'd turned to her fiancé and waited, sure that he'd agree, but there was always that little practical side of her mind that worried he might say no.

"It's a blend of both our worlds and very beautiful. I look forward to learning more about you and your family."

Deacon's words warmed her heart. If possible she'd marry him today. "Then it's settled."

"Not the flowers or the food," Sadie spoke up, waving her arms to gain their attention. "But if it's okay, Phaedra and I would like to put together a menu. We'll run it past you then we'll have the cooks at the Red Neck Bar and Grill make it."

Lyn clapped her hands together and looked at the crowd of friends and family who loved her. "I am so fortunate to have all of you. Thank you for being part of my life." She walked to Deacon and placing her arm around his waist, she let her head rest against his chest.

"Do you have a preference? Food?"

"Well, I fell in love with the food we had in Greece. If they can put it together, I'd like Greek food with lots of bread and wine."

"We will ask them. Isn't one of the waitresses from Athens? Seems to me she grew up there. She's not Greek, but she must know how to cook the food."

"Flowers," Lyn reminded her.

"I love them all. Blue flowers, I don't care what kind."

"I'll take care of the flowers. It will have to be simple there are not a lot of places to put flowers at the cliff, but I'll put together a bouquet with blue flowers in it."

"Thank you, all of you."

"Now the date." Kimi stood in front of her, hands on hips, tapping her foot as if impatient.

"Can we get all of this done in a week?" Deacon asked; his brows knit together.

"Just like a man, always in a hurry for the wedding," Phaedra said laughing.

"Give us two weeks. I'm sure the wedding dress will need to be altered for Lyn. She's taller and thinner than I was."

~ * ~

"Perfection." The warmth of the sun melted into Lyn's flesh. Small feather white clouds dotted a cerulean blue sky and a gentle breeze wafted through the tall grass. Even though the blue hibiscuses were the predominant flower, the land still smelled of sagebrush and heat.

"Are you nervous?" Kimi stood beside Lyn, a bride maid's bouquet made from blue hyacinths and white angels breath in her hand. Her dress was a soft baby blue color and the heart shaped bodice accented her breasts and the tight waist to a flowing skirt made her look absolutely sexy.

"Strangely no." Thoughts of her handsome groom simmered in Lyn's head. Vividly, she recalled his touch, the smile in his eyes when he looked at her. She loved him more than she could ever think possible.

175

"Good, because I'm nervous for both of us." Kimi stepped from one foot to the other. Suddenly she turned to face Lyn. "What do you think of Mak?"

"You like him, don't you? Is he your mate?" If he was, Lyn hoped they'd figure it out sooner than later. She knew her little sis, and she also knew Kimi had wondered for years if there was someone out there for her.

"I don't know. Everything has been focused on you and your problems. We haven't been able to see where our feelings will take us. I know it will take a little time, but you know me, I'm impatient. I want the everything now, not tomorrow."

Lyn's heart slipped to her stomach. She had never wanted the focus on her and she'd never thought sea monsters would try to destroy her life. "I'm so sorry. I didn't mean..."

Kimi shook her head. "Don't feel sorry. I don't want to worry you today. It's your special day and I want you to be happy. You look so beautiful."

"Back at you. I don't think I've ever seen you so drop dead gorgeous." Lyn paused a moment, thinking about Kimi's words. "All right then but I wish I hadn't been the center of attention for so many days." Lyn watched the others approach, her mother and father, brothers and cousins, and extended family.

"It's about time. You ready?"

She inhaled a long, deep cleansing breath. "I am." A slow rhythm of the drums permeated the surreal setting high atop Infinity Cliff. Boom, boom, boom...

She watched Deacon and Brody walk to the top of the cliff then stop beside their great grandfather who wore ceremonial apache attire. He looked so wise and proud. The backdrop behind them set the stage for the apache wedding.

Next to Niagel stood Sean McClain, ready to read them more traditional vows.

Niagel nodded, signaling Kimi to walk forward. Then Lyn's father stepped beside her. The McKennas had found their places and sat in chairs Balor had been brought to the site of the wedding. Balor sat down in the back and when he turned to look at her, he looked like a proud papa, the smile on his face so broad.

The slow beat of the drums signaled her walk down the aisle. Lyn's heart pounded, her breath raced. She swallowed hard, knowing how important these next few moments were to her. This was her life and Deacon was about to become her husband.

Her father stopped in front of both priests.

Niagel nodded.

"Do you give your daughter's hand in marriage?" Sean McClain asked.

Her father nodded.

She stepped forward then handed her bouquet to Kimi, knowing her life was about to change forever.

The ceremony proceeded in a blur. Then they were saying the Apache prayer, repeating the sentences after Great Grandfather spoke them.

"Now you will feel no rain, for each of you will be shelter for the other. Now you will feel no cold, for each of you will be warmth to the other. Now there will be no loneliness, for each of you will be companion to the other. Now you are two persons, but there is only one life before you. May beauty surround you both in the journey ahead and through all the years. May happiness be your companion and your days together be good and long upon the earth.

"Treat yourselves and each other with respect, and remind yourselves often of what brought you together. Give the highest priority to the tenderness, gentleness and kindness that your connection deserves. When frustration, difficulties and fear assail your relationship, as they threaten all relationships at one time or another, remember to focus on what is right between you, not only the part which seems wrong. In this way, you can ride out the storms when clouds hide the face of the sun in your lives -- remembering that even if you lose sight of it for a moment, the sun is still there. And if each of you takes responsibility for the quality of your life together, it will be marked by abundance and delight."

They turned to Sean and he read a passage from the bible. Then went on to ask if each would accept each other is sickness and in health, for better or poorer. The ceremony went on and Lyn tried to remember each part. Before she knew it they were giving each other rings and he pronounced them husband and wife.

"Now that you are wed in both the Apache way as well as the Protestant, you may kiss the bride," Sean said with a grin on his face.

Deacon lifted her veil. She moistened her lips, waiting for the soft touch of his lips upon hers. He was gentle but chaste. Nothing like the scorching kisses of other times, but they spoke a promise of a future, of good times to come.

"Everyone rise, I present Mr. and Mrs. Deacon McClain."

A round of applause followed. Deacon took her hand in his as they walked down the aisle. She smiled at her friends and family who had found their way to the top of Infinity Cliff to witness their vows.

Then Brody and Kimi followed them as they formed a receiving line.

Her father and mother were first before taking their places in the line.

Her mom gave her a big hug, "You're beautiful, Lyn. I love you and it doesn't seem as if I can say the words enough. I hope you have a long and happy life with your mate."

"Thank you." Beaming from the inside out, she hugged her mom back then her father.

Mak was in line, gave her a hug and a huge grin, "You two were meant for each other."

He stepped beside Kimi, taking her hand in his.

A long, low rumbled shook the cliff.

Then the sky darkened and a strange noise filled the air. A whirling tunnel descended from the dark clouds and thunder roared across the top of the cliff. A spiral of lightning hit the ground near the receiving line.

Lyn screamed and Deacon wrapped his arm around her as he pulled her to the ground. More lightning hit the earth and wind swirled around them. She tried to see, but Deacon's arms covered her.

Demonic laughter filled the air, sending chills slithering down her spine. What in God's name was happening? It sounded as if the world was coming to an end or were the sea monsters here trying to kill her again? Would they never stop?

"Oh my God, Deacon. What's happening?"

As suddenly as it began, it stopped. Deacon pulled Lyn to her feet in time to see a swirling funnel cloud lift two people into the air and devour them.

"Kimi!" Lyn screamed.

About the Author
achristay@aol.com

Born in Medford, Oregon, novelist Christine Young has lived in Oregon all of her life. After graduating from Oregon State University with a BS in science, she spent another year at Southern Oregon State University working on her teaching certificate, and a few years later received her Master's degree in secondary education and counseling. Now the long, hot days of summer provide the perfect setting for creating romance. She sold her first book, Dakota's Bride, the summer of 1998 and her second book, My Angel to Kensington. Her teaching and writing careers have intertwined with raising three children. Christine's newest venture is the creation of Rogue Phoenix Press. Christine is the founder, editor and co-owner with her husband. They live in Salem, Oregon.

Other books by Christine Young
Available at Rogue Phoenix Press

Catching Meara
Book One in the McKenna Clan Series

Meara Thorton was a feisty, world-class computer hacker—cornered by the FBI and shockingly given the chance to be their newly acquired technical analyst. Brilliant and intuitive, yet aching with the loss of everyone she has cared about, her restless heart led her to discover a love she fought and a world she didn't know could possibly exist.

Sweet Sexy Sadie
Book Two in the McKenna Clan Series

From the first time Sadie's eyes met those of Brody McKenna in the hot Sierra Madre Mountains, theirs was a potent attraction—not gentle, slow, and easy, but hot, hard, and all-consuming. The daughter of a dysfunctional family, Sadie had dreams no man could wrench from her with hot sex and an all-consuming passion. She'd challenge this alpha male with all the strength she possessed. But her red hair, fiery temperament, and indomitable spirit obsessed Brody...and he knew he had to find a way to show her he was more than he appeared and convince her to make a life with him.

Sweet Misbehavin'
Book Three in the McKenna Clan Series

Cast adrift after fleeing the home of Jokul, the ice demon, Atantsi, a firestarter, grew to womanhood as she moved through time to keep the demon from finding her. Though stubborn and courageous, she was ill prepared to use powers she had not been taught. Her first sight of the intoxicating Carr McKenna left her breathless, and her second encounter gave her hope for a future she never thought she had.

A playboy, a second son and a shifter, a man who thought his life would be carefree, Carr McKenna was shocked to discover the woman he'd paid as an escort is a firestarter who is running for her life. He is the leader of all the McKennas around the world and that he has multiple powers. His passion for Margo and the need to defend her might cost him his life as well as hers.

Highland Honor
The first book in the Highland Series

Willfully stubborn, innocently courageous, Callie Whitcomb braves a journey through the treacherous highlands to the Macpherson castle. Callie flees from an unwanted marriage as well as her ruthless half brother. Naively she believes Colin MacPherson, the head of the clan, is loyal to her father and will give her sanctuary, protecting her from the vile plans that have been made for her.

As hard and as unyielding as the winter storms that sweep through the countryside, Colin is irresistibly drawn to the impetuous beauty who has magically appeared on his doorsteps. Despite his vows of revenge against her father, she stirs his passion as well as his sense of justice...but to love her would violate all his vows of revenge.

Highland Magic
The second book in the Highland Series

Throughout the Highlands she is known as Keely, the witch woman. She is a great healer-a woman whose dreams come true. Ian MacPherson is a man who puts honor, loyalty and duty above everything. Their lives are entwined when Ian is sent by the Scottish King to bring Keely to trial for witchcraft. He is attacked and left for dead, but Keely rescues him. When he wakes, he discovers he has no memory. As he remembers his lost past, Ian finds that his need to protect the woman who has saved his life eclipses his duty to his king and country. He is a man torn between honor and duty to his country and the woman he loves.

Highland Song
The third book in the Highland Series

With her white-gold hair and azure eyes, Lainie MacPherson is as wild and untamed as the rugged Scottish Highlands where she was raised. Lainie vowed to avenge her rape. Recklessly, she defies English laws and the man who raped her puts a bounty on her head. The man who is sent to bring her to Edinburgh sets a dangerous trap. With nothing left to live for the beautiful Scottish spy steals the sealed documents the English soldier has tempted her with.

When the exquisite temptress takes the bait and runs off with not only the forged documents but the purses of the men in the tavern, Aaron Slade vows to hunt her down and bring her to justice, never dreaming she will tame his jaded soul. When Aaron discovers the truth about the tempestuous woman who stirs his passion to the point of madness, he dares not love her, but desires her with all his soul.

Dakota's Bride
The first book in the Lakota/Pinkerton Series

When Emma St. John received her brother's letter imploring her to escape her stepfather's vengeful scheme and to trust Dakota Barringer with her life, she was willing to chance it. But the handsome, brooding riverboat owner Emma found in Natchez a danger of another kind. For Emma soon found herself surrendering to an unrelenting desire.

Raised by the Sioux when his parents were killed, Dakota had been betrayed once before by a white woman. He wasn't about to trust another, especially one claiming that her stepfather, a powerful U.S. senator, had framed her as a murderess. But he couldn't let Emma's intoxicating effect on him. Now Dakota would risk his very life to protect the innocent beauty who had seduced him with her tender love.

My Angel
The second book in the Lakota/Pinkerton Series

A BEAUTY IN BUCKSKINS
When her father decided to send her to a finishing school back East, Angela Chamberlain refused to be confined to stuffy drawing rooms. Instead, the daring spitfire who could shoot like a man and ride like the wind longed for a life of adventure and romance—and she knew exactly who could give it to her. Devil Blackmoor was a hired gun with a dangerous reputation. But Angela was willing to go to the ends of the earth to capture the handsome devil's heart.

A DEVIL IN DISGUISE
He'd come to America looking for excitement, but Devil Blackmoor got more than he bargained for when he encountered a beautiful rebel who answered his kisses with a wild innocence that touched his very soul. Yet standing between them were more obstacles than either ever dreamed. For Devil had strapped on a gun for the wrong man. And that made Angela his enemy. Now he'll have to choose between his duty and the woman he loves more than life.

The Locket
The third book in the Lakota/Pinkerton Series

The year is 1894. Seeking revenge for crimes against his family, Misha Petrovich follows a path that leads straight to Ariel Cameron's boarding house in Mist Harbor, Oregon. A family heirloom in Ariel's possession leads Misha to believe she is guilty. The locket has been handed down to the oldest girl in the Petrovich family for generations. Ariel is innocent of wrong doing, but her father is not. Misha is torn by his feelings for Ariel and his need for restitution against her father. Knowing that the relationship between them is fragile, Misha does everything in his power to protect Ariel's father. His efforts are to no avail when her father is shot. Ariel comes to realize Misha's steadfast courage and determination to protect her and her father despite what has happened to his family. Ariel's love and devotion heals Misha's heart.

The Talisman
The fourth book in the Lakota/Pinkerton Series

Running from a marriage that lasted one night, Dr. Moriah McKeown discovers the land she has settled on is coveted by determined and lawless men. Yet the proud young woman who once vowed never to abandon her home has second thoughts when her adopted children are threatened. Her only recourse is to enlist the aid of a dark, dangerous gun for hire.

Haunted by the past and a betrayal he will never forgive, Ian Civanovich uses his fast gun and his reckless courage to forget the faithlessness of a woman in his past. He will trust no female—nor will he rest until the threat hovering over Moriah McKeown is put to rest.

Forever His
The fifth book in the Lakota/Pinkerton Series

Struggling to come to terms with the part she played in Jacob St. John's death, Etta Barringer resigns from Pinkerton Agency and seeks peace and solace in a Rocky Mountain Cabin.

Jacob has vowed to discover the reason Etta has betrayed him, sold him out to his enemy and left him for dead.

Isolated in their cabin, they discover their love for each other and learn to trust. But the trust is shattered when Jacob learns she is married to his sworn enemy; the man who left him in the desert to die.

Allura
The first book in the Twelve Dancing Princesses Series

Allura McClellan is horrified by her father's decision to take out an ad in the Times awarding her to the man strong enough and smart enough to win her hand and uncover her secrets. She's an intelligent young woman who takes great delight in the freedom allotted to her by her father. She's well aware that marriage would effectively curtail the adventures she's shared with her sisters and cousins.

Hunter Gray is nothing like the other men who've arrived to vie for Allura's hand in marriage and everything that goes along with it. However, he is the first to refuse to concede defeat and pursue her despite her attempts to disguise her true appearance. It's her temperament that is of more concern to him than her looks. Hunter has worked all his life with the hope of someday owning his own land. Now that it looks like there's a very real possibility that everything he's ever wanted is within reach nothing is going to deter him – including Miss Allura's disagreeable disposition.

The Wager
The second book in the Twelve Dancing Princesses Series

Amorica Hepburn was sent to London to find a husband. Finding a man was the last item on her agenda. With her two cousins, Amorica wagers she can dissuade her suitor before the others. Despite her efforts she discovers a chemistry that cannot be denied. Suddenly she is the arrogant man's wife, pledged to a marriage neither desire. But swept off to his ancestral home above the Dover cliffs and into his strong embrace, Amorica is soon possessed by a raging passion for the husband she had vowed to despise…

Damian Andrews couldn't afford to trust the emerald-eyed spitfire who happened upon his secret. Amorica's hatred of all men of his kind only inflames the war that rages between them. Still, he can not control the intense desire his stubborn bride inspires, or make her surrender to his will until he has conquered the headstrong beauty on the battlefield of love…

A Marriage of Inconvenience
The third book in the Twelve Dancing Princesses Series

A REGAL BEAUTY
When the duchess decides to wed her to a wastrel and a fop, Ravyn Grahm takes matters into her own hands and declares her engagement to another man. Instead of fessing up and telling her great aunt what she has done, she goes through with the pretense. Aric Lakeland is the bastard son of an earl and has a dangerous reputation. But Ravyn is willing to do most anything to keep the duchess from discovering the lie.

A DEVIL-MAY-CARE SMUGGLER
He'd bought land in America, looking to put down roots and end his life of adventure, but Aric Lakeland got more than he bargained for when he encountered a beautiful heiress who made a promise she didn't want to keep. But the promise could not be undone and standing between them were more obstacles than either ever dreamed. Aric had made plans to spend the rest of his life in America and that was at odds with Ravyn's plan of living in England and running her father's estate. Now, he'll have to choose between his dreams and the woman he loves more than life.

Highland Sunrise
The fourth book in the Twelve Dancing Princesses Series

He Made Her An Offer...

Life has thrown Christel McClellan some experiences that could have devastated a less determined woman. Beautiful, self-assured and fiercely independent, she is trying to forget the loss of her stillborn child. But is the child alive?

She Couldn't Deny...

Life is carefree for Ryder MacLaren who loves to see what is on the other side of the sunrise. Laird of Clan MacLaren, he is wealthy, handsome and happily unencumbered...until stunning Christel McClellan enters his life. When he hears her story, he believes the child she thought dead has been sold to a wealthy buyer.

Storm's Passion
The fifth book in the Twelve Dancing Princesses Series

SHE MADE A PROPOSAL...

Life strikes Storm Graham a shattering blow when she learns her father has bartered her to a man she detests. Storm is beautiful, self–assured and fiercely independent, and refuses to be a pawn in her father's schemes, yet she can find no way out of this bargain made in hell. Going on the offensive she asks the wealthiest man on the eastern coast of England to marry her, never believing she might fall in love.

HE TRIED TO REFUSE...

For Hadden Johnston life has provided everything he ever wanted, including a sanctuary for homeless children. He is wealthy, handsome and happily unencumbered...until stunning Storm Graham marches into his life and proposes a marriage of convenience. Yet this type of marriage to a woman who inflames his senses is far from acceptable. If he's going to be tied down, he will move heaven and earth to have this woman warming his bed.

Rebel Heart

HER REBEL SPIRIT DEFIED HIS OUTSIDERS SOUL... She was velvet and silk, eyes the color of a summer storm and amber hair. Victoria DeMontville, because of a promise and a codicil to her father's will, was forced to marry one man to protect her from another. She hated Cameron Savage with a fierce passion. But to hold on to her genetic research and find a cure for the deadly Signe virus, she must pretend to love the enemy at her door, come with weapons of fire to melt her icy heart...

HIS OUTSIDERS TOUCH IGNITED RAGING PASSIONS... He wore a mask, disguised as the Phantom, a true legend come to life. Even as war and debate over new genetic research engulfed them all, he would find his greatest adversary in the beauty who'd branded him an outsider and barbarian, the woman he was born to possess, his soul mate.

A St. Patrick's Day Tale
by
Christine Young, C. L. Kraemer, Genene Valleau

Tumble through time…

…to Ireland in 1817, when tensions are high between Protestants and Catholics and faey people guide the fate of villagers. A lovely Catholic lass stumbles upon the weakly ritual fisticuffing between Irish lads. She falls into the lap of a handsome young Protestant. Family ties, grudges, and two conniving faeries threaten their budding love. But the faeries outsmart themselves when they hijack a time machine that has mysteriously appeared in their forest and are whisked to…

…Eugene, Oregon in the 20th century, amid a property feud between the local faeries and night elves. The conniving faeries from Olde Ireland try to stir up more mischief. However, a warrior gnome convinces the magic folk to control their own destiny, and forces the intruding faeries to take refuge in the time machine again, spinning their way toward…

…A modern day castle in western Oregon. An eccentric inventor is determined to reclaim his wayward time machine and save his beloved wife from her latest misadventure. If only they can travel safely past the black hole…

A Valentine's Anthology

The Lending Library-a fantasy by Christie L. Kraemer
Faeries try to fit into the human world when the forest where they make their home is destroyed by a mysterious enemy.

Chasing Rainbows-a contemporary romance by Genene Valleau
An eccentric aunt, an inventive uncle, a mother who wears poodle skirts, and a brother who wears pearls provide a hilarious backdrop for the courtship of a young woman who yearns for a "normal" family.

The Gift-an historical romance by Christine Young
A man and a woman on opposite sides of the Civil War get a second chance at love after one final battle returns soldiers to their war-torn homes to rebuild their lives.

Writing as AnnChristine

Safari Moon

Solo St. John, a wildlife photographer, is preparing for a trip to Alaska. Suddenly, Solo finds women of all sorts invading his privacy, his home and his office, all cooing nonsense words and blatantly throwing themselves at him. Solo doesn't know why, and he has no idea how to rid himself of the persistent women. He finally decides to beg a favor of his best buddy Nyssa Harrington.

In love with Solo for the past ten years and knowing he doesn't return her feelings Nyssa doesn't want to talk to Solo. She knows if she accepts his phone call, she will not be able to resist the temptation to hope again.

A Valentine's Anthology
Sharks byAnnChristine

Will Lily and Jacob, best friends forever, find love or will they discover friendship is not enough for a relationship to take the final step into marriage.

The House on Berkley Street by K. J. Dahlen

When Serenity is asked to find the truth in a forty-year old tragedy, someone in the town of White Oak, Texas doesn't want the truth told. Can they stop her before she finds out what they have kept hidden for so long?

The Placebo Effect by Solstice Stevens

First, there was the poison. Then, there was a four story jump and the basketball hoop. Jessamyn Hamhill's life has been one validation attempt after another . . . until now.

www.ingramcontent.com/pod-product-compliance
Lightning Source LLC
Chambersburg PA
CBHW060220180626

46813CB00007B/2898